A LITTLE SH

One cowboy stared at Slocum, his fists still doubled for action. ''An' just what the hell is that, city slicker?'' he asked heatedly, swaying slightly on his feet after too many rounds of beer . . .

Slocum took one quick step closer to the cowboy and launched a looping right hook into his jaw, hearing his knuckles crack against jawbone just as the cowboy went reeling backward, slamming into the wall before he slid down to the floor on the seat of his pants, glassy-eyed.

Slocum turned quickly to the other man. ''The next one's yours unless you hightail it out those bat-wings,'' he snarled, drawing back for another blow with his hand stinging in the aftermath of his first powerful punch.

The cowboy dropped his hands to his side. ''Don't want no trouble with you, mister. It was 'twixt me an' Claude.''

''Claude's gone to sleep for a while,'' Slocum said. ''Now get out like the lady asked you to or you'll be taking a little nap on the floor there beside Claude . . .''

JAKE LOGAN

BLOOD IN KANSAS

JOVE BOOKS, NEW YORK

BLOOD IN KANSAS

A Jove Book / published by arrangement with
the author

PRINTING HISTORY
Jove edition / June 1998

All rights reserved.
Copyright © 1998 by Jove Publications, Inc.
This book may not be reproduced in whole
or in part, by mimeograph or any other means,
without permission. For information address:
The Berkley Publishing Group, a member of Penguin Putnam Inc.,
200 Madison Avenue, New York, New York 10016.

The Penguin Putnam Inc. World Wide Web site address is
http://www.penguinputnam.com

ISBN: 0-515-12291-2

A JOVE BOOK®
Jove Books are published by The Berkley Publishing Group,
a member of Penguin Putnam Inc.,
200 Madison Avenue, New York, New York 10016.
JOVE and the "J" design are trademarks
belonging to Jove Publications, Inc.

PRINTED IN THE UNITED STATES OF AMERICA

10 9 8 7 6 5 4 3 2 1

BLOOD IN KANSAS

1

It was a town crawling with profit-seekers and gamesmen, by all appearances, and when John Slocum rode into Fort Smith on a breezy fall day, he also noted a goodly number of dangerous types, if that sort of thing could be judged by the way a man carried a gun . . . or by the way he kept his eyes on his surroundings, always cautious, watching everyone else as if he expected a bullet in the back. It was that same breed of caution that kept Slocum alive, and he recognized it among other men, the wariness, ever watchful of strangers, seemingly ready for anything including gunplay. It was not the use of guns that brought him to Fort Smith this fall. He had an appointment with a pretty lady, which was Slocum's preference when he had a choice. Beautiful women were his passion, the cause of many of his mishaps and some close brushes with death, while at the same time bringing him the greatest moments of happiness he'd known since before the war.

On this particular occasion he came calling with a gift, a present from a friend up in Springfield. He'd never cared for the state of Missouri all that much, and he was glad to be headed west again, although by a circuitous route, a detour southwest in order to make the acquaintance of a raven-haired beauty by the name of Myra Belle Shirley, owner of a Fort Smith saloon. And the gift he brought was worthy of her attention, a magnificent dagger almost a foot in length, imported from the Orient long ago with an ivory handle inlaid with gold. Intricate carvings made the ivory a piece of artwork, and the knife was said to be worth a small fortune, an antique with a long history, belonging to a Mongol warlord hundreds of years in the past. The gift was being given by a generous benefactor, Bradford Thomas of Springfield, for favors granted by the lovely Myra Shirley while Bradford was in Fort Smith.

Bradford was a cousin to Heck Thomas, a U.S. Deputy marshal serving under the authority of Isaac Parker, known throughout Indian Territory and the Western Judicial District of Arkansas as "The Hanging Judge." According to a story Slocum had read in the *Springfield Gazette,* Parker had thus far hanged ninety-one men for assorted crimes, and in one instance he'd ordered a hanging for six men simultaneously, drawing crowds and newspaper reporters from as far away as Kansas City to watch the grisly event. Slocum knew a little about Judge Parker and his ghoulish executioner, George Maledon, from personal experience. He'd helped a longtime friend and lawman bring three wanted men to the Fort Smith stockade. Before Slocum could ride out of town a trial date had been set, and by the time he got to Denver on the train, all three men had been hanged. Judge Parker wasted no time meting out his brand of justice.

Brisk winds whipped through the thick forests blanketing the hills on both sides of the road into Fort Smith as Slocum rode within sight of the stone fort. Bright fall colors turned every leaf into a fluttering display of nature's changes as gusts rippled through swaying branches, releasing more leaves with each breath of swirling air. Maples a flaming red or gold, and oak leaves from deep orange to every imaginable shade of brown, drifted across the road in front of him. He'd always enjoyed fall more than any season. Its changes were more dramatic than spring's, even though spring was almost equally spectacular—blooming wildflowers, new leaves in the forest and spring grasses turning the landscape various hues of green.

He had a romantic side that had nothing to do with a need for a woman, and he oftimes thought he might be in love with nature itself more than any bounty awaiting him underneath a woman's skirt. He'd noticed it more as he got older: an appreciation for open country, or the High Lonesome as some mountain men called it, just about any place where civilization had not left its mark. With so much westward expansion he knew the day would come when there were no more open spaces where a man could ride for days without encountering another human being. He hoped that day was beyond his lifetime since he experienced so much peace in empty land.

At times he thought of himself as two people: one a man who needed the attractions of city life, good whiskey and the best cigars, a soft bed and an even softer woman, other a man who needed to be away from all of the comforts afforded by larger towns. In truth, it was most often a woman that brought him to a town. His natural urges did more to lure him away from a wilderness or a mountaintop than any need for comforts of another kind.

The place he sought was aptly called, according to Bradford Thomas, the Powderkeg, known for its habitation by men of often intemperate disposition who frequently settled their differences by employing exploding gunpowder. It hadn't sounded like a place for a beautiful proprietress; however, Bradford had given Slocum assurance that Myra could handle herself with desperate men. He'd said she was a crack shot with a pistol, and the gift Slocum was bringing her would only assist Myra in keeping order at close quarters.

While this had sounded a mite on the doubtful side when Slocum first heard it, he'd known Bradford long enough to rely on his opinions in these matters. Over the years Slocum had sold a number of blooded racehorses to Thomas, and they knew each other well. Bradford's first cousin, Heck Thomas, was one of the most feared U.S. marshals in Indian Territory, and Slocum sensed the same determination and fearlessness in Bradford. It was enough to know Myra Shirley had Bradford's respect when it came to tough situations. Bradford's respect was not to be taken lightly.

Rows of low wood buildings sat along the edges of dusty streets east of the fort, some with signs advertising their wares or services. A strip of saloons lay to the south, perhaps with a certain amount of forethought, as far away from the fort and the offices of lawmen as practical. At the far end of this same road he saw a crudely painted sign proclaiming that the building beneath it was indeed the Powderkeg. As it was late afternoon, men with guns were about on boardwalks along the saloon district, eyeing Slocum warily as he swung his bay Remount Thoroughbred stud toward the establishments peddling whiskey, a more or less natural direction for John Slocum most of his life. Where whiskey was sold there were usually plenty of women.

He noticed several men paying particular attention to the swell of the Colt .44 underneath his coat, the stock of the rifle booted below his left leg under a stirrup leather, and his shotgun poorly concealed in the middle of his bedroll—butt plate and sawed-off barrels showing on either end. His guns were a form of advertisement not unlike the signs nailed to the roofs of these saloons, telling those who noticed that he came to town heavily armed. His cross-pull holster was the most meaningful to men who understood guns and gunplay. A man who wore a cross-draw rig was either crazy or very fast, depending upon how long he'd had it buckled around his waist. Quick draws were tricky with a gun on the far side of a man's belly, requiring dexterity as well as lightning-fast reactions. Slocum knew all about the advantages too, leaving a trail of grave markers when he was given no choice but to prove he knew how to make a fast cross-belly pull.

One gent in particular was giving Slocum the eye as he drew rein in front of the Powderkeg. The man wore a gun tied low on his left leg, a sweat-stained gray flat brim hat, and stovepipe boots in need of blacking, and was leaning against a porch rail.

"Howdy, stranger," the cowboy said, giving Slocum a single nod, a mix of suspicion and curiosity written across his face, a frown knitting his forehead slightly.

Slocum came stiffly from his saddle seat, touching ground with trail-weary legs without taking his eyes from the man who spoke to him. "Howdy," he replied, tying off his reins at the rail before he began loosening the bay's cinch just enough so the horse could blow.

"Whereabouts you from?" the cowboy asked. It was a question with no trace of friendliness.

"This here saddle, of late," he said, annoyed by the man's inquisitive nature.

The cowboy's face hardened somewhat. "You sure as hell do carry a bunch of guns, mister. Couldn't help but notice."

Slocum's annoyance was becoming outright anger. He

turned to the cowboy. "There's times when I use 'em to kill folks who ask too many goddamn questions," he said evenly, so there could be no mistaking his warning.

The cowboy hardly batted an eye. "That's mighty tough talk, stranger. An' this is one hell of a bad place to test your luck unless you're real fast."

Tired of the banter, he stepped up on the boardwalk in front of the Powderkeg, taking a glance above a pair of swinging doors leading into the place before he spoke to the man again. "I may not be all that quick with a gun," he said, staring hard into the cowboy's eyes, "but I don't hardly ever miss what I'm aimin' at, and I reckon that's why I'm still alive. Now, if you're done with all the questions, I've worked up a powerful thirst. That saloon yonder has got just what I need, only I'm standing here answering a bunch of goddamn questions when the answers ain't none of your business."

The cowboy grinned mirthlessly. "You step inside that place an' you'll find plenty of boys who'll oblige you with a test of who's the best with a gun. It's early yet, but I'll wager there will be one or two who'll see if you're as good as you claim to be."

"Never claimed to be good," Slocum answered, realizing now that this cowboy posed no immediate threat of reaching for his pistol. Slocum could see it in his face. He started for the bat-wings and spoke over his shoulder. "I said I hit what I aimed at, is all. Can't remember the last time I missed."

He went inside carefully, pausing near the door frame so as not to be outlined by daylight coming from the street until he knew what waited for him there.

Three men stood at the bar, watching him in a mirror on the rear wall above stacks of clean glasses and bottles with an assortment of labels. Over to his right a lone cowboy slumped in a chair, hunkered over a shot glass full of amber liquid. Behind the bar a bald man with gartered sleeves nodded to Slocum politely.

"Come in, mister," the barkeep said. "This is a friendly place an' we serve the best whiskey an' beer in Fort Smith."

Slocum glanced through a smudged front window to check on his horse before he replied. "I'll have a glass of your best bourbon, Kentucky sour mash if you have it, and then I'd like to send word to Miss Myra Belle Shirley that I'd care to see her as soon as it's convenient."

The barkeep reached for a branded bottle behind him and a shot glass. "Miss Shirley won't be in for a spell. You'll have to come back after sundown. Maybe eight or nine this evenin'."

"Suits me," Slocum replied, easing over to a vacant table in a room smelling of old cigar smoke, unwashed spittoons, and unwashed men. As was his habit, he took a chair against the wall so he could see the room and the doors.

The barman came around his bar to bring Slocum a glass full of foul-smelling fluid, clearly not the sour mash he'd ordered.

"This is the best we got," he said, carefully placing the glass before Slocum. "That'll be two bits."

Slocum took silver from his pocket. "Sounds high for three fingers of moonshine colored with tobacco juice, but I'll pay for it. Just to cut the dust from my throat."

"That's real Kentuck' sour mash," the barkeep protested as he swept Slocum's quarter off the tabletop with a fleshy hand.

"Save your speech. I know the difference."

The bartender scowled. "If you're callin' me a liar I'll have you thrown out of this place, stranger. I done told you its Kentuck' sour mash whiskey."

Heads turned at the bar when drinkers heard the exchange.

"I didn't call you a liar," Slocum replied quietly, but with an edge creeping into his voice. "Maybe you simply don't know the difference. As to throwing me out of here, it'll be mighty hard to do without plenty of help. But I'll save you all the trouble by leaving on my own until Myra gets here. A friend of hers sent me and I aim to talk to her. I have something for her from Springfield, and I doubt she'd be happy if she found out you suggested I leave her place without making the delivery I'd promised to make."

An uneasy silence lingered in the Powderkeg for a time, until the barman shook his head. "I ain't givin' you no damn apology till I find out who you are, mister. That fancy suit coat an' silk vest don't impress me none. We get more'n our share of high rollers in this place. You can stay, so long as you shut your mouth about this not bein' Kentuck' sour mash."

"I won't say another word about it," Slocum replied, picking up his glass while everyone was watching. Then he leaned over a nearby spittoon and poured his drink out with an added dash of ceremony.

He got up slowly, meeting the defiant look in the barman's eyes with a stare of his own. "I'll be back around nine. Tell Miss Shirley that John Slocum asked for her and that I've come with a gift from Bradford Thomas."

Slocum left the Powderkeg, pausing near his horse to see if the nosy cowboy was still there. He found the porch empty and without further delay, he mounted his bay and headed for a livery stable to arrange for keeping the horse overnight. Fort Smith had never been known as a friendly town. However, today's events had left a really bad taste in Slocum's mouth that had nothing to do with the rotgut whiskey he'd paid for.

2

Myra Belle Shirley wasn't what Slocum expected in a frontier town like Fort Smith. He'd been told by Bradford Thomas she was a beauty, but nothing could have prepared him for the vision of loveliness Slocum saw the moment he entered the Powderkeg a few minutes past nine that night.

The place was crowded, shoulder-to-shoulder drinkers lining the bar and every chair at half-a-dozen tables occupied. It was a small saloon by Slocum's standards. He was accustomed to some of the biggest and best in places like Abilene, Dodge City, Fort Worth, and San Antonio, or Denver's largest gambling parlors, which in turn could not compare to the elegance of places in New Orleans or Saint Louis. Here the air was thick with cigar smoke and the stink of men too long without bathwater, making it that much harder to believe a woman in an expensive black evening gown, cut low in front to reveal a generous bosom, stood behind the bar serving drinks to cowboys, better-dressed drummers, and a few farmers clad in overalls, about as odd a mixture of patrons as any Slocum had ever seen. Slocum knew without being told that the black-haired woman was Myra. She fit the description Bradford had given perfectly.

There was no space at the bar, and Slocum hesitated, unwilling to elbow his way between the gun-toting men crowded around Myra and holding glasses of whiskey and mugs of foamy beer. For a while he simply stood there near the swinging doors with his back to the wall admiring her. Her skin was like the handle of the ivory dagger he'd brought her from Springfield—so smooth, the color of fresh milk, without a trace of a blemish he could see from afar. Her teeth were a brilliant white, and when she smiled her entire face beamed. He wondered if it was a practiced smile for the benefit of her customers.

Several men scattered around the room demanded Slocum's close attention before he walked away from the wall, men with guns in deeply notched holsters tied down low for a minimum of resistance during a fast draw. He read some of the faces after he'd had a good look at their guns, to see if he recognized any as being hombres he'd tangled with someplace before. But he saw no one he remembered, and his memory for that sort of thing was good, one of the finer points of staying alive in the West, where a face or a name could spell sudden death if a careless man crossed paths with the wrong shootist.

Slocum relaxed, watching Myra again, wondering how many men had known her intimately, wishing he'd been one of that number, or been given a chance to join them. She had a tiny waist. He took a guess at her age—less than thirty, probably closer to twenty-five or six, since women who frequented saloons had a tendency to age quickly. She had small hands with delicate fingers, and he was reminded of what Bradford had told him, that she was a crack shot with a side arm. Her fingernails were painted a glossy red, as were her full lips. Her obsidian hair was done up in ringlets framing a face with high cheekbones, a touch of rouge below them, which only set off her fine chisled features.

What a woman, he thought, with a keener understanding of how Bradford Thomas could remember her so vividly. In any city Slocum had ever visited, Myra would certainly be one of the most stunning women around. A tiny place like Fort Smith, with fewer than three thousand townfolk, seemed an unusual place to find a woman such as her.

A slender blond waitress scurried back and forth among the tables carrying a tray laden with whiskey and beer. She was very pretty too, in a plain sort of way, lacking rouge or lip paint or a fancy dress that might show off her curves. An experienced eye like Slocum's could almost see through her shapeless cotton skirt and flour-sack white blouse. Underneath her home-sewn garment a full body was hidden, with ripe young breasts about the size of his fist, and there was a suggestion of rounded hips swaying back and forth when the girl hurried to and from the bar. Slocum liked what he saw in both women, although they were as different as two women could be, one a diamond in the rough, the other a perfectly cut and polished stone.

When he was sure no one was paying attention to him, notwithstanding the few furtive glances from patrons when he'd entered the place, Slocum stepped away from the wall and sauntered toward the bar with his coat unbuttoned, just in case a sudden need arose for a gun. He found a narrow spot between a drummer in a derby hat and a farmer where he could signal either the bartender or Myra. The din of conversation was loud enough to make it difficult to be heard for a time, until the bald barkeep noticed him from the corner of his eye as he was filling a mug of beer from a wooden keg spigot. As soon as he spotted Slocum, he stopped filling the mug and turned to Myra.

"That's him, Miss Shirley," he said loudly above the

ruckus made by so many voices. "Yonder's the feller I told you about when you came in."

Her attention was immediately drawn to Slocum while she put two glasses of whiskey on the bar. Her smile widened. She took time to collect a handful of coins from a pair of drinkers, and then she came over to Slocum.

"I'm Myra Shirley," she said, her voice almost husky. "Tell me who it was that sent you. Sam said he couldn't remember for sure."

Slocum returned her smile and touched the brim of his hat as he replied. "Bradford Thomas at Springfield. I'm John Slocum. I brought something for you, a gift from Bradford, but I can see you're busy now. Maybe later you'll have some free time."

"A gift?" she asked with a note of disbelief. "Why would Bradford send me anything?"

"Can't say for sure, ma'am, but he did mention something about you showing him some special favors while he was in Fort Smith and he felt he owed you."

Her smile was joined by a pretty pink blush filling her cheeks with color. "What sort of gift did he send, Mr. Slocum?"

"I'd rather not say. I'd much prefer to show it to you sometime when you aren't so busy."

Myra glanced around the packed room. "It'll slow down some in a few hours, when some of these boys get so drunk I order them to leave. I won't tolerate a noisy drunk in my establishment or a troublemaker, and damn near everybody in town knows it. I'm sorry I can't take off now to see . . . whatever it is Brad sent me. I do wish he hadn't given me anything." Now her eyes sparkled with mischief. "Can't you tell me what it is? I'm nearly dying of curiosity."

"I think Bradford would want me to show it to you first,"

he replied. "Besides, it'd be mighty hard to describe. In a manner of speaking, it's a work of art, but that wasn't all the artist had in mind. It's very old, he told me—several hundred years, I think he said—and it came from the Orient—"

A disturbance in a corner of the saloon ended what Slocum was telling her. He looked over his shoulder at two angry men squared off with fists doubled as if they meant to start swinging at each other. They were shouting cusswords, while other patrons quickly cleared out of the way.

Myra's smile evaporated. "Excuse me a moment, Mr. Slocum, while I attend to a little housecleaning," she said, turning toward the end of the bar, lifting the hem of her gown to keep from tripping on it as she hurried around from behind the bar toward the troublesome men with her mouth drawn in a hard line.

As a gentleman should, he pushed away from the bar to help her if things got out of hand, following Myra to the table where the pair of cowboys taunted each other with insults and shaking fists.

"That's enough, boys!" Myra cried before she got to their table, and the sound of her voice completely silenced the room. "Take it outside or I'll settle it for you!"

All eyes in the place were on Myra. One of the men involved in the disturbance gave her a scowl. "Ain't no woman gonna tell me what to do," he said. "This is between me an' him."

Myra placed her hands on her hips. "This is your last warning, mister," she told him. Then she aimed a finger toward the door. "Take it outside. Now!"

Neither man seemed convinced, staring at her, apparently unwilling to back down from a woman in front of a roomful of men witnessing the affair.

Slocum decided it was time to intervene. Myra's barkeep had made no move to back her play, standing quietly behind the bar as if he hadn't noticed the disturbance at all.

"You heard what the lady said," Slocum remarked in a low growl, stepping around Myra so he looked both men in the eye. "Get outside, and do it real quick or you won't like what's gonna happen."

One cowboy stared at Slocum, his fists still doubled for action. "An' just what the hell is that?" he asked heatedly, swaying slightly on his feet after too many rounds of beer.

To save Myra from having to do anything herself, even if she did know how to use a gun as Bradford had said, Slocum took one quick step closer to the cowboy and launched a looping right hook into his jaw, hearing his knuckles crack against the jawbone just as the cowboy went reeling backward, slamming into the wall before he slid down to the floor on the seat of his pants glassy-eyed.

Slocum turned quickly to the other man. "The next one's yours unless you hightail it out those bat-wings," he snarled, drawing back for another blow with his hand stinging in the aftermath of his first powerful punch.

The cowboy dropped his hands to his sides. "Don't want no trouble with you, mister. It was 'twixt me an' Claude."

"Claude's gone to sleep for a while," Slocum said. "Now get out like the lady asked you to or you'll be taking a little nap on the floor there beside Claude."

The murmur of hushed conversation came from corners of the saloon as the second cowboy headed for the swinging doors with his head down, trying to hide his embarrassment.

Myra spoke. "I can handle my own problems, Mr. Slocum, but thank you for what you did just now."

"I'll drag the sleepin' gent outside," he said, bending

down to grab Claude by his shirt collar. Claude's head lolled to one side, but his eyes were slitted open.

Everyone in the Powderkeg was watching as Slocum pulled the half-conscious man across the floor, then outside. A few voices spoke quietly about what had happened.

When Slocum shouldered back through the swinging doors he came face to face with the blond waitress. Conversation had resumed throughout the saloon. The girl smiled at him as Myra was coming over. Slocum grinned and tipped his hat to the waitress before Myra arrived. Myra noticed his attention on the girl.

"This is Pearl, Mr. Slocum," Myra said, giving Pearl a flickering glance. "Pearl always was taken by handsome men, and it appears she's got her eye on you."

"That ain't so, Miss Myra," Pearl protested, blushing deeply as she avoided looking at Slocum now. "I was only bein' polite."

Slocum laughed. "You're a pretty girl, Pearl," he said in a gentle voice. "I wish I'd brought *you* a priceless work of art."

Myra was watching Slocum closely. "You pack one hell of a wallop with those big hands. Thanks for what you did. If you can come back in a couple of hours, I'm dying to see what Bradford sent me. He shouldn't have sent anything so expensive, a priceless thing."

"I'll be back," he said. "And I'll see if I can find a good bottle of Kentucky sour mash someplace, maybe at the general store across from my hotel."

Myra smiled. "We have good whiskey, only Sam isn't supposed to sell it to anyone other than my special guests. He keeps it under the bar. Good whiskey is hard to come by in Fort Smith, so I keep a tight rein on the best stuff." She tilted her head in a playful way. "I'm looking forward to spending some time getting to know you, Mr. Slocum, after things quiet down around here.''

"I'll come back around eleven," he promised, wondering if getting to know Myra might land him in her bed. He also noticed Pearl was staring at him, listening closely to what he said. "I can show you what Bradford gave you," he told Myra. "You won't believe your eyes when you see it. He told me it's worth a lot of money."

He walked out into the darkness in a better mood despite the pain in his sore knuckles. Claude lay sleeping on the porch of the Powderkeg as though his own fuse had just been blown out.

Walking slowly up the street, Slocum heard raucous laughter and out-of-tune piano music coming from some of the other saloons he passed. The saloon district was crowded tonight.

At a cross street he turned west, strolling toward his hotel under a sky filled with stars as he heard the rumble of hooves near the fort. Half-a-dozen heavily armed men with stars pinned to their chests galloped away from the stockade, rifles bristling in their hands.

"Trouble somewhere," he muttered, wondering if Judge Parker had sent out another batch of warrants for lawbreakers across the river in the Indian Nations. Indian Territory was changing, according to what Slocum read about it in the newspapers, as the Hanging Judge sent more and more possemen after outlaws who had previously been running roughshod over cattlemen and travelers crossing Indian reserves set aside by the government to keep the Indians peaceful. And according to newspaper accounts, Judge Parker's iron determination to bring peace to the territory was making its mark, taking a heavy toll on outlaw gangs operating out of the Nations.

He thought of Myra again as the posse galloped across Fort Smith to vanish into the darkness. "I'll bet she's one hell of a filly to ride," he told himself, wondering if he'd get the chance to find out first-hand.

3

A sixth sense warned him someone was following him, and he looked over his shoulder. He caught only a glimpse of a moving shadow before it disappeared between two buildings, a dry-goods store closed for the night and an office advertising a buyer for beaver pelts and other "tanned hides." It puzzled Slocum to know he was being followed when he had no enemies here, unless he counted Claude, who was still recovering on the porch of the Powderkeg from a fist to the jaw, or maybe Claude's erstwhile friend. For a moment Slocum stood in a shadow below the slanted roof of a blacksmith's shop, searching the darkness for any sign of the person behind him, his right hand near the butt of his .44. When he saw nothing else, he made his way carefully toward the Cattlemen's Hotel, pausing often to make sure no one was behind or in front of him.

He crossed Main Street and entered the lamplit lobby, where an older woman noticed his arrival over a pair of spectacles halfway down her nose.

"Good evenin', Mr. Slocum," she said, smiling.

"Evenin', ma'am," he replied, heading for a stairway leading to his second-floor room with a final glance out a

18

hotel window to see if anyone was watching him. The street was empty.

He unlocked his door and closed it behind him, deciding to wait in his room until the appointment with Myra at eleven. He struck a lucifer to a lantern's wick, keeping the lamp turned down low before he opened a window. Slocum hung his coat and hat on wall pegs and unfastened his gunbelt, looping it around a bedpost. His traveling gear lay in a corner. He fetched two cigars from his war bag and all that remained of a half-pint of whiskey—only a few swallows of decent bourbon, not the best but passable for a traveling man. Propping feather pillows against the headboard, he rested with a lit cigar while sipping whiskey. He let his mind wander back to Myra, deciding he'd been too long on the trail without a woman.

A soft knock on his door brought him upright with a start, for he hadn't heard footsteps in the hall. He reached for his gun and got off the bed quietly, wondering who would pay him a call in Fort Smith . . . unless it could be Myra, although he hadn't told her where he was staying and the town had three hotels.

He crept to the door. "Who is it?" he asked softly, ready for anything, holding the pistol in his fist with his finger on the trigger.

A quiet woman's voice replied. "It's Pearl, from Miss Myra. She told me to bring you this bottle of Kentucky corn an' to say she's sorry she can't make it tonight, on account of she's got a gentleman caller. I asked the lady downstairs for the number of your room, after I found the right hotel."

Slocum lowered his gun and unlocked the door. Pearl stood in the darkened hallway holding a fifth of labeled whiskey, and he could see the girl was nervous. "Come in," he said, standing back to admit her. "I was just about to head down to Myra's to keep our appointment."

"I hadn't oughta go in a stranger's room," she replied as she handed him the bottle, smiling a little. "It wouldn't be the proper thing."

He grinned and gave her a shrug. "I don't think anybody's looking, but you can suit yourself, Pearl. Tell me again why Myra can't meet me."

Pearl took a hesitant step to the threshold and stopped in the doorway, clasping her hands together in an anxious gesture, her eyes moving quickly around Slocum's room before she looked at him again. "A gentleman acquaintance arrived unexpectedly an' she said to tell you she was real sorry, that it couldn't be helped, an' how much she was lookin' forward to seein' what you brought her from Springfield, only she can't make it tonight."

"I can give it to her tomorrow morning, I reckon, although I was in need of a woman's company for a spell. It wouldn't be at all improper if you stayed just long enough to have a small drink of this whiskey, would it? We can talk a moment or two, if you can spare the time."

"I really shouldn't, Mr. Slocum."

He thought he detected a note of uncertainty, as though she might be persuaded if he pressed her on it. Years of experience in the seduction of women gave him a feeling for this sort of thing. "Just one drink and a bit of pleasant conversation, Miss Pearl. That's all I'm asking for. I'm sure you can tell I'm a little disappointed to learn Myra can't be here, and you could help me get over feeling so let down, seeing as you're every bit as pretty as she is."

Pearl blushed deeply. "You're just sayin' that. I know I ain't as pretty as she is. Why, she's nearly the prettiest woman I ever saw in my whole life."

Slocum uncorked the bottle and offered it to her. "She is a very beautiful woman, wearing beautiful clothes, her hair done up in a fashionable way, with lip paint and rouge. You'd be just as pretty if you wore a fancy gown like hers."

Pearl was still undecided, glancing briefly at the bottle as her cheeks continued to color. "It's real nice of you to say it, only I know it ain't true." She smiled and took the whiskey. "I don't reckon it'll hurt if I have just one tiny sip an' stayed a minute or two." She came in and he closed the door behind her as she lifted the bottle to her lips.

"Take a chair next to the window," he suggested. "I'll sit a proper distance away on the edge of the bed. That way you'll know I have only honorable intentions."

Pearl crossed the room and sat on the edge of a wooden chair near the windowsill, keeping a watchful eye on Slocum as he went to the mattress and sat down. It was another hopeful sign when she took a second swallow of whiskey before she gave him the bottle.

He tipped the bottle back and drank thirstily, admiring the girl's pretty face while he swallowed a burning mouthful of good sour mash. "This is good stuff," he told her as a breath of night wind lifted curtains beside the window, making a fluttering sound.

"Miss Myra keeps it hid," she said. "It's only for her very best customers an' friends. To tell the truth, I ain't all that fond of the taste of any distilled spirits, only they do make me feel good sometimes, if I don't drink too much of it."

Slocum judged the girl was very young. He didn't intend to ask her age at a time like this. "Whiskey does make you feel good," he said. "And I confess I do like the taste. I'll confess to another thing, if it don't seem out of line. I'd like to see what you looked like in a dress like the one Myra was wearing. In fact, I'd like it so much that I'll buy you one tomorrow morning, if a nice dress can be found in Fort Smith.''

Pearl's brow furrowed. ''Why would you do that, Mr. Slocum? Why would you be so generous to somebody you never met?''

He offered her the bottle and leaned back, resting against the headboard with a grin on his face. ''Let's say I'm a man of means, someone with money, and I enjoy seeing pretty ladies in nice dresses. That's all it is. I sell expensive race-horses to wealthy men and I make a nice profit. Nothing wrong with sharing a little of my money, is there?'' It was only partly true, what he said about having money. He had made a nice profit on the horses he'd sold to Bradford Thomas.

She drank, watching him, looking so pretty in the soft light from the lantern. ''Maybe not,'' she said finally, ''so long as you don't expect nothin' in return.''

''If you gave me a smile, that would be enough,'' he said in a matter-of-fact way. ''Of course, I'd have to see what you looked like in the dress if I paid for it.''

Pearl giggled. ''That would be okay, of course,'' she said in a little girl's voice, ''only I couldn't wear a dress cut too low in front, if you know what I mean.''

''Why's that?'' he asked, playing along.

Her face became a fiery red. '' 'Cause I ain't got as much on top as Miss Myra, that's why. I shouldn't be talkin' about such things with a man, should I?''

''I don't see any reason not to. Besides, a big bosom isn't what makes a woman beautiful, and it looks like you've got enough underneath that cotton blouse to fill out a dress very nicely.''

''Lordy,'' Pearl exclaimed, clasping a hand over her

mouth to suppress another giggle. "Talk like this just ain't proper at all."

"Didn't mean to offend you, Pearl. All I said was, you've got plenty of bosom to fill out an evening gown. You are a very pretty woman, only you don't dress to show off how pretty you are underneath those loose-fitting clothes."

She took another swallow of whiskey. "Would you really buy me a dress without expectin' anything in return?"

"I would. I'll do it first thing tomorrow when the stores are open. You can pick out the one you want, and a handbag to match. I'd even buy you some lip paint and rouge, if you want me to."

"This don't make any sense," she told him, looking him in the eye. "All I'd have to do is wear it for you?"

"That's all."

"I'm not sure I believe you, Mr. Slocum. It sounds too good to be true, that you'd buy me a dress an' a handbag just to see me dressed up nice."

He reached into a front pocket and withdrew a money clip full of bank notes. With Pearl's eyes glued to what he was doing, he counted out twenty dollars and left it on the mattress. "If you doubt me, take the money tonight. We can meet at the dress shop in the morning, if you'll tell me where it is and what time to meet you."

Her eyes rounded like saucers as she looked at the money. "My goodness," she gasped. "A dress wouldn't cost that much."

"I only meant to prove I'm a man of my word, and that I'd trust you with the money until we found just the right gown."

Pearl took a gulp of whiskey this time, while he put the rest of his money away.

"The only thing I'd ask," he continued casually, "is that

you pick one that shows off your nice figure. I'd want it to be cut down in front, like Myra's.''

"I'd be too embarrassed," she answered, still eyeing the stack of currency, "but I suppose I could make an exception if it's what you really wanted."

He wondered if she knew by now what he really wanted. "I would have to insist that it showed some of what you've got. I don't think that's asking too much, is it?'

"I reckon not," she replied softly, "only I figure you'll be real disappointed. I was borned with . . . small breasts. They ain't like Miss Myra's at all an' I'd look silly in a dress that showed how little they are."

"They look just the right size, only I can't really tell all that much about 'em with that blouse you're wearing. You keep it buttoned all the way to the top."

"Mercy me!" Pearl declared. "It sure is gettin' hot in this room." She fanned herself with a hand. Then she smiled. "If I open one or two buttons, you wouldn't think nothin' bad about me, would you? All I'd be doin' is showin' you how little my breasts are, just a peek at the tops of 'em, so you'll know."

"That would be fine, Pearl, and I certainly wouldn't think any less of you for opening three or four buttons, just so I'd see exactly what sort of dress you'll be needing tomorrow."

She still appeared hesitant, and drank from the bottle one more time. "I don't suppose it'd hurt anything," she said a moment later. "Can't nobody see me up here, an' nobody's gonna know I done what you asked on account of buyin' me a new dress. That'd be the reason, if I undone some buttons. . . ."

His prick made a wet, sucking sound every time he drove it deeper into her slick, hot cunt. Pearl moaned, digging her nails into his back, her arms and legs quivering as he lay between her thighs pumping his cock in and out of her hungry mound. Sweat dampened the bedsheets in spite of a cool fall breeze blowing through the window.

"Oh, John!" she exclaimed, arching her spine off the mattress when he went deep. "You're hurting me. . . ."

He kissed her lightly on the ear, still pumping steadily, only a few inches of his cock buried inside her for now. "It'll stop hurting in a minute," he whispered, feeling his balls rise as her warm juices heightened his excitement.

She gasped when another inch of prick entered her. "It . . . does . . . feel . . . good," she panted, thrusting to meet his pounding shaft. "It's . . . very hard . . . to explain."

She'd given in to his advances reluctantly, and only when the whiskey did its work had he been able to convince her to take off all her clothes. "No need to explain," he now told her gently, with her ripe young breasts rubbing up and down across his chest hair. She had a beautiful body, youthful, but perfectly proportioned.

She trembled from head to toe, clamping her legs around him in a viselike grip, clawing the small of his back, then his shoulders. She increased the rhythm of her thrusts when he put more cock between the lips of her cunt, and suddenly she began driving toward a climax, slamming her silken mound onto the base of his prick.

Only seconds later she let out a muffled scream and went completely rigid underneath him, shaking violently, wagging her head back and forth on the pillow, while she tried to stifle the noises coming from her throat.

Pumping harder, he felt a familiar warm sensation in his testicles as they prepared to explode. He wasn't sorry at the moment that Myra Shirley couldn't make their appointment this night. Pearl had proven to be a wonderful substitute, and there was always another night he could devote to Myra.

4

At dawn he awakened with an odd feeling something was wrong, a sensation he couldn't attribute to anything in particular, just an awareness of things being different somehow. He sat up in bed and rubbed his eyes, noticing a slight headache after too much of the excellent whiskey Pearl had brought him.

He was alone in bed and couldn't remember the girl leaving, and as his gaze wandered around the room he saw his valise and war bag in the middle of the floor, their contents scattered all over. Slocum was suddenly wide awake, jumping off the bed, for he knew now what had happened . . . he'd been robbed.

"Damn," he whispered savagely when he found his pockets had been emptied and the bundle of crimson velvet containing the ancient Mongol dagger was missing. "The bitch took everything."

He'd been carrying almost a thousand dollars, money from the sale of two Thoroughbred stallions to Bradford Thomas in Springfield. It was a fortune by any man's standards, especially his own. Pearl had seemed so young and innocent, only now he knew better. It had all been an act, a ploy, to rob him. He stared down at his pants, pockets turned inside out, silently cursing his own stupidity. He couldn't go back to Denver without the money, nor would he consider leaving Fort Smith without getting the dagger back to give to Myra. Bradford had trusted him to make the delivery, and he'd start looking for it and stay on its trail until Hell froze solid to keep from breaking his word to an old friend.

"Can't believe I was so easily fooled by the little bitch," he mumbled, pulling on his pants and then his socks and boots before he selected a clean shirt from what lay scattered across the hotel room floor. "I'll find her . . . and when I do I'll bet she was in cahoots with somebody. She wasn't smart enough to think of this on her own. She's got a partner somewhere, a gent who put her up to this, probably somebody who heard me tell Myra about the knife."

Or had Pearl simply overheard their conversation and notified an accomplice? He wondered about it as he buttoned his shirt and strapped on his gunbelt, deciding to take along a .32-caliber belly gun he carried hidden under his shirt for those times when extra firepower at close range might be needed. He tucked the gun inside his shirt, growing madder by the minute as he thought about how easily he'd been fooled. He looked down at the bulge of his cock where it lay next to his leg, poorly concealed by the tight fit of his pants. "You keep gettin' me in trouble," he said, addressing the organ.

Before he left his room he fortified himself with several strong pulls on the half-full bottle of whiskey, more to steady his nerves and cool his anger than anything else. He was a thousand dollars poorer on account of a woman this morning, and missing a valuable work of art that had been entrusted to him. He'd be damned if he'd let it rest until he found Pearl and whoever was in on the robbery with her, and when he found them he swore an oath to make them regret their actions.

He stormed out of his room and locked the door behind him, pulling his Stetson low over his eyes as he stalked angrily down the hallway. His first order of business was to report the theft to local peace officers. Then he had to inform Myra about what had happened, and see how much she could tell him about the girl who worked for her, who she knew, where she lived, how long Myra had known her, and who a likely accomplice might be. It had to be someone Pearl knew intimately. Surely Myra would know who that might be.

"Don't know much about her," City Marshal Dave Watkins said in a rather disinterested way. "Can't even tell you her last name for sure. She came to town a couple of months ago with this down-at-the-heels gambler by the name of Dan Willis. Willis was a card cheat, an' not all that good at it either. Big tall feller who carried a derringer in his boot an' had extra cards up his sleeves. Best I remember, he left town without Pearl about two or three weeks ago. Pearl told Myra Shirley she needed a job real bad, an' because Myra can be so good-hearted, she gave Pearl a job as a waitress. Never heard of her stealin' nothin', or any complaints from Myra 'bout her work habits."

Watkins rubbed his ample belly and got up from a creaking chair behind his desk. "I got to go get some breakfast, Mr. Slocum. Feel like I'm damn near starved. I'll look into this robbery after I get a bite to eat. I'll go down to that boardin'house where Pearl was stayin' to see if she's still there . . . only, you an' I both know she ain't gonna be, not after she robbed you of so much money an' that ol' knife you said you was carryin'. Pearl probably cleared out soon as she left your room. Maybe somebody saw her leavin' an' I can try to follow her tracks . . . if she left any. Far as I know, she didn't own no horse. When Willis left town he took their old wagon an' the harness horse. Seems I recall somebody told me he was headed down to Texas. Maybe he was gonna send for Pearl when he found a card game he could win someplace.''

Slocum was furious. Watkins's attitude toward the robbery was almost indifference. ''I'll go down to the boardinghouse if you'll give me directions,'' Slocum said, steeling himself to keep from saying what was really on his mind. Watkins was an overstuffed, swaggering man who obviously had a high opinion of himself. He had a waxed handlebar mustache, and a nickle-plated gun on his hip that didn't look like it had seen much use, other than regular cleanings. His badge had a high polish on it too, and it was easy to see he was proud of it, and his position.

''It's south of the railroad tracks,'' Watkins replied. ''Big sign on an old two-story house sayin' it's got rooms for rent. You can't miss it if you head south across the tracks. Lady who runs the place is named Darlene Sims.'' He hoisted his gunbelt higher around his waist, then gave what might pass for a grin. ''I'm sure you know you're wastin' your time. If Pearl took your money an' the knife, she's long gone by now.''

''Could she have gotten on a train?'' Slocum asked as he went to the office door, hesitating, unable to remember hearing a train whistle last night.

Watkins wagged his head. ''Nope. Just one train runnin' in either direction nowdays. One comes in the mornin' headed west, down to the Texas border at Texarkana. Late afternoon one comes through headed east. If she robbed you last night like you say, she didn't leave town on no train 'cause there ain't been one yet an' the first one comes at around ten o'clock this mornin'. She would have to be crazy to be waitin' around for a train with a pocket full of stolen money.'' The marshal frowned. ''You say it was nearly a thousand dollars? Why the hell would you be carryin' that much money?''

''I sold some horses,'' Slocum replied, swinging out the door impatiently, striding toward the railroad tracks.

Watkins came out on the porch. ''Musta been a hell of a lot of horses,'' he said to Slocum's back.

Mrs. Sims gave him the news he'd been expecting when he got to the boardinghouse.

''She left real early this mornin', mister. Kinda strange the way she was actin', like she was in a real big hurry. She paid me all her back rent an' said somethin' important had come up, an' she had to leave town. There was this feller waitin' for her outside, right over yonder under that big oak tree. It was dark an' I couldn't hardly see him, but he was leadin' an extra horse for her. She put on a pair of britches an' took everythin' she had in a couple of burlap bags. Why, she nearly ran off my porch to git on that horse, like she was in a real big hurry to git wherever they was goin'.''

''Did you happen to see which way they rode?'' Slocum asked.

The old woman frowned, rubbing one temple with her fingertips as if it would help her remember. ''Seems like they rode off thataway.'' She pointed due west, toward a bend in the Arkansas River. Beyond the river lay Indian Territory.

He tipped his hat. ''Thank you, ma'am. I sure wish you could recall what her friend looked like.''

"It was dark, mister, maybe four in the mornin'. I'd just got up to make biscuit dough fer my boarders. Wasn't payin' no particular attention, to tell the honest truth, since she up an' paid me all her back rent."

"I'm obliged," he told her, starting down her porch steps.

"There was one thing," Mrs. Sims said, pausing, staring off blankly for a moment. "The feller was ridin' a dun horse, a big yeller buckskin color. Showed up real good in the dark on account of its color."

"That could be a help," he said, hurrying across her yard, although he knew this part of the country had plenty of Spanish-bred buckskin horses. It might turn out to be good news. If one of them was riding a horse with Spanish barb blood, it wouldn't be blessed with a great deal of speed, in most cases. A Thoroughbred like the one Slocum rode stood a good chance of catching up, if he could only pick up their trail.

One last bit of business stood in his way before he began looking for the tracks of two horses. He had to tell Myra what had happened, and inform her that he was going after her knife and his money.

As he stode quickly toward the business district to inquire about the location of Myra's house, he thought back over what he knew about Indian Territory—the Nations. The only law in the territory came from U.S. marshals patrolling the various sections set aside for different Indian tribes, and there were precious few deputies to cover so much wild, empty country. He'd be on his own, for the most part, looking for Pearl and the man who helped her rob him; however, that was no concern to Slocum. Over the years he'd done a considerable amount of man-hunting alone and in most respects, he preferred it that way. Mounted on a good horse, he could cover more ground than most men, and when he found who he was looking for, he knew he could handle himself, even against long odds. He'd faced long odds most of his life, and it could be safely said he was accustomed to it.

Myra Shirley's house stood in a grove of maple trees on the northeast side of town, a better residential district where folks who could afford bigger and better houses lived. He knocked on her door even though it was early, not yet eight in the morning.

For some time he got no answer to his tapping, until he knocked harder, more insistently. Minutes later he heard a woman inquire, "Who's there?"

"John Slocum, ma'am. Sorry to bother you but I have to ask you a few quick questions, and I'm afraid I've also got a bit of bad news."

"Bad news?" Myra opened the door clad only in her dressing gown, a filmy silk garment revealing more than a mere suggestion of her curves.

"Afraid so, Miss Shirley. I was robbed last night and the gift I brought you from Bradford Thomas was stolen, as well as a sizable amount of money, nearly a thousand dollars."

Myra brushed hair away from her face. It was obvious she had still been in bed when he knocked. "Do you have any idea who did it?"

"Yes, ma'am, I do. The girl who worked for you named Pearl. You sent her to my room last night with that bottle of whiskey."

Myra's face darkened. "I didn't send her to you. She said she was sick, an upset stomach or something of the kind, and I gave her the rest of the night off. She came to your room?"

"With a bottle of Kentucky sour mash, the good stuff.

She told me you sent it over with your apologies, that you couldn't see me last night because you had a gentleman caller arrive in town unexpectedly."

Now Myra's expression turned angry. "It's a damn lie!" she snapped, beckoning Slocum into her foyer. "I didn't have a caller last night. When you didn't show up around eleven, I only assumed you'd gotten tired after a long trip and gone to bed. I never sent her to your room or anything of the kind."

Slocum walked in with his hat in his hand. "Tell me what you know about Pearl. I already found out she cleared out of the boardinghouse where she was staying, and that some gent on a dun horse was waiting for her. Mrs. Sims told me Pearl paid all her back rent and left in a hurry, about four this morning."

"The rotten bitch," Myra whispered, not bothering to close the front of her silk robe. "After all I did to help her. The lying little bitch said she felt sick."

"I reported it to Marshal Watkins. He didn't sound like he was in all that big a hurry to go after her, after them, so I plan to go myself. Mrs. Sims says she thinks they headed for the river, and I reckon that means they crossed over into Indian Territory. I'm going after them."

"Who's the man who was with her? Did Mrs. Sims know who he was?"

"She said it was too dark to see him. All she saw was a big buckskin horse."

Myra appeared to be thinking. "There was this halfbreed who showed a lot of interest in Pearl. Everybody called him by his nickname . . . something like Scar Face, or Cut Face, because he had this big scar running down his cheek. My bartender, Sam, told me he had a mean reputation and he didn't want him at the Powderkeg. Come to think of it, he

was there last night. Left right after you did. Sam said someone told him the breed was a murderer, a killer for hire, and
that he was wanted by the law up in Kansas. Ask Marshal
Heck Thomas about him. I think they questioned him a few
times about incidents over in the Nations. All I remember
about him is what they called him, and I think it was Cut
Face something or other. Heck will know."

"I'm grateful for the information," Slocum said, wheeling for the door. "I'll find them, and when I do I'll get your
gift back as well as my money."

"What was it?" she asked as Slocum went out on the
porch.

"Bradford sent you a very old dagger inlaid with gold.
It came from Mongolia, he said."

"A dagger?" she asked as he hurried down the steps.

There wasn't time to explain.

5

Heck Thomas was a bulky sort, with a beard and mustache, two pistols belted around his hips. He was younger than his cousin Brad, and heavier. Slocum knew him by reputation, that he was dedicated to his job with the Marshals' Service and relentless when on the trail of lawbreakers. He sat in a tiny office at the fort compound listening to Slocum tell his story without saying a word until Slocum finished.

"If it's the same jasper, he goes by Cut Face Jake Willow. His Cherokee pappy named him, after he got cut in a knife fight with an Arapaho stealin' Cherokee horses one night. Jake is a mean son of a bitch . . . ornery as hell to handle, 'specially when he gets drunk. He's good with a gun, so they tell me. I brought him in for questionin' a few times, when somebody over in the Nations lost some livestock or got killed. We wired authorities up in Kansas about him one time. They said they had plenty of suspicions, only they couldn't prove nothin' on Jake for sure.

"Folks is scared of him. He's big. Rowdy with his fists or with a knife. Some claim he's a hired assassin, a back-shooter who'll kill just about anybody fer money. U.S. Marshal Sam Ault over in the Western District of the territory says Jake trades guns to the Kiowa and Comanch' fer buffalo hides, only they can't catch him at it. He can be real smart. Hard to follow on horseback. He knows how to hide his trail.

"The trouble with your story is, we got no witnesses who saw Jake Willow with that girl after she robbed you. All we can do is keep an eye out for her, 'cept we're real short-handed as of now. Sent six men up to Osage country last night. We got a report there's a gang of trail-cutters stealin' off big herds on the Chisholm. The Goodnight outfit lost over a hundred head of steers crossin' Osage land, an' if you know anything about them Osages, they're pretty peaceful now. Mostly beggars. The last time I was there they looked like they was half-starved. It's a gang workin' that section, probably renegades or white outlaws who know we can't cover every goddamn square inch of the Nations with so few men. Judge Parker issued a warrant an' ordered six men up yonder to put a stop to it. Leaves us real short-handed, like I said."

"I'm going after Jake Willow and the girl myself," Slocum said.

Thomas scowled. "You can't go takin' the law into your own hands, Mr. Slocum."

"No law says I can't look for what's mine and if I find it, bring whoever took it back here to stand trial."

"Officially, I gotta tell you it's a legal matter when a robbery gets committed. But unofficially, I'll tell you this. If you go lookin' for Cut Face Jake Willow you'd best be real careful, an' if you find him you better be good with a gun. He ain't got many soft spots, so they say."

Slocum stood up, glancing at his bay stud tied to a rail in front of the marshal's office. "I can take care of myself, Marshal. By the way, your cousin Bradford said to tell you hello if I saw you. I just rode down from Springfield, after I sold him some racehorse breeding stock.''

Thomas grinned. ''Brad's plumb crazy when it comes to good horses. Always was that way. We don't see each other much, but if you see him afore I do, return the howdy-do an' tell him I'll get to Springfield one of these days.''

''I'll pass the word along,'' Slocum said, reaching for the doorknob to let himself out.

''Another thing,'' Thomas said, before Slocum went out. ''You better know how to read horse sign. If they cross the river like Miz Sims said they did, Willow will be hard to track. He's part Indian, an' they learn things 'bout hidin' a horse's prints most white men never know.''

''I've had a little experience,'' Slocum replied. ''Don't know how I'll stack up against this Jake Willow, but unless he owns a horse with wings, I'll find his sign somewhere.''

Thomas chuckled, then gave Slocum a look of appraisal. ''You've got all the appearance of a city boy by the way you dress, but I can tell by the way you carry yourself you're more'n that. I reckon I had you figured wrong at the start.''

''I've got trail clothes at the hotel, Marshal. To tell the truth, I only dress up like this when I'm on business, like the trip to Springfield. I've spent most of my life in denims and buckskins, and for a while, a Confederate uniform.''

The marshal was still grinning. ''I could tell by the way you talk you was a Southerner.''

''Georgia. I try not to think about the war much now.''

''Good luck lookin' for Cut Face. But don't forget what I said about him. He'll double back on you if he knows you're on his trail, an' the son of a bitch won't make it no fair fight, if what I hear about him is true.''

''It's mighty hard to find a fair fight, Marshal,'' Slocum

said. "Most of 'em I've been in have been one-sided as hell, and I was usually on the short side of things, or that's the way it always seemed. I appreciate your warnings, but I'll manage. A few times I've been in some close scrapes and it looked like I was about to cash in my chips. Some way or other, I've always found a way to win. Ever since the war got started, I've been a real hard man to kill. That, or I've been real damn lucky a bunch of times."

He rode back and forth along the riverbank looking for hoofprints made by two horses. If Jake Willow was as smart as Heck Thomas said he was, he'd ride upstream or downstream before they came out, to make his trail harder to find. Slocum was accustomed to seeking difficult trails, made by careful men, Indians or men of any color. Sooner or later, even the most cautious hombres made a mistake. Patience was the key to tracking them, and Jake Willow had a woman with him, a girl too young to know the ways of nature, where a broken tree limb or bent grass was like a signpost telling an experienced eye which way they went.

He was clad now in buckskin leggings, worn at the knees, a Cheyenne gift from long ago when he'd helped a young warrior find medical attention after a bloody encounter with a Crow raiding party. Slocum also wore a bib-front shirt and Sioux moccasins, an unusual combination of attire worn by red men and white. His hat shielded his face from the sun, its brim pulled low in front, and in his bedroll he carried a buckskin jacket, should the weather turn cold. He brought along jerky, a canteen, and coffee beans for a tiny coffeepot. The rest of his gear was weaponry: his rifle, his shotgun, both pistols, and a Bowie knife. His saddlebags contained a generous supply of ammunition for each of his guns. If the girl and Jake Willow led him to hell and back, he was as ready as he could be to track them down.

An hour later he was briefly filled with hope when he found two sets of hoofprints roughly half a mile north of town, but as he swung down to examine them, his hopes fell. Both were made by mules—a narrower print than those made by a horse, less width at the heels. But as these were the only prints he could find, he followed them for a spell, noting they were fresh, and in short order he crested a wooded hill and sighted a man in a flop-brim hat leading a pack mule, riding another mule.

With the hope that this traveler might have seen Willow and Pearl, he urged his bay to a lope, riding up on an old man in tattered clothing, sporting a gray beard, looking half wild and some days away from his most recent bath.

"Howdy, stranger," the old man said as Slocum reined to a halt beside him. He carried a pistol in his belt, although he made no move toward it, as if he didn't expect trouble.

"Howdy," Slocum replied. "Just wondering if you happened to see a man and a woman headed west this morning. The man would be riding a buckskin horse, if he's the one I'm looking for, and the woman is young, with blond hair."

The old man scratched his tangled beard. "I did see two riders a couple hours back, toppin' hills to the north of me. I ain't got real good eyes no more, but one of them hosses was a yeller color." He stuck out his hand. "Ben Adams is the name."

Slocum accepted his handshake. "John Slocum. Could you tell me what direction they were headed?"

"West, same as you an' me. How come yer askin'?"

"They stole something from me. I aim to get it back and if I can, I'll escort them back to Fort Smith."

"Are you a lawman? Don't see no badge."

"I'm only doing what I have to do to get my belongings and my money from 'em. Nothing official, but if I can, I'll haul them to Judge Parker's court to stand trial for robbery."

Adams grunted, gazing north a moment. "Whoever they is, they'd better know how to handle themselves out here. This ain't friendly country for a greenhorn, or a woman."

"The man I'm after supposedly knows his way around this neck of the woods. I was told his name is Cut Face Jake Willow."

"Holy Christmas!" Adams exclaimed. "Ain't nobody warned you 'bout Cut Face?"

"Marshal Heck Thomas said he could be dangerous, that he's suspected of several killings and cattle theft."

At that, Adams chuckled knowingly. "There's a hell of a lot more'n suspicion to it. Cut Face ain't right in the head, if'n you know what I mean. He's plumb crazy, an' he'll shoot a feller in the back same as look at him. If you want some advice, I'd turn back an' let the law handle it. Cut Face knows this Injun Territory like the back of his hand, an' he's got some friends who're tougher'n coffin nails. Anybody with good sense who knows anythin' about Cut Face Willow steers wide of him."

Slocum scanned the northwestern horizon. "Since you seem to know that much about him, tell me where you figure he'd be headed if he rode west."

"That'd be easy. He'll aim fer Talequah, just this side of Fort Gibson. There's this outlaw roost in them hills. Call it the Crow's Nest. Ain't hardly much there 'cept a tradin' post an' a few buffalo-hide-buyers' tents. You wouldn't be crazy enough to go there, would you, stranger?"

"If that's where I can find Jake Willow and my stolen property."

"You'd have to be plumb outa your mind."

Slocum examined the packs tied to one mule's back. "Which way are you headed, Adams?"

The old man shrugged and had a rather sheepish look on his whiskered face. "The Crow's Nest. Seein' as you said you wasn't no lawman, I'll tell you the truth. I got whiskey to trade fer a few buffalo skins. It's ag'in territorial law to sell or trade whiskey to an Injun, but I do it. A man's gotta make a livin' somehow. I used to run traps in this country, afore they made it a bunch of Injun reservations. They took my livin' away when they give it to them savages."

Slocum knew what he wanted from Adams. "Mind if I tag along? I'll keep you out of it as soon as you show me where it is."

"Ol' Cut Face would scalp me sure as hell if he knowed I showed you to the roost."

Slocum was running out of patience, knowing that Willow and the girl were getting farther away. "I'd just follow you anyway, Adams. May as well enjoy each other's company for a spell."

Adams shook his head. "You ain't got no idea what you're askin', Slocum, but if you're determined to git yourself killed, it ain't no skin off my nose."

"When we get to this Crow's Nest we'll part company some distance away. Nobody will ever know you took me there, or that you told me I might find Willow and his woman."

Adams gave the hills a sweeping glance. "Suit yourself on it, Slocum. It'll be your hair he takes if you meet up with him an' his pardners. They's one hell of a bad bunch to tangle with an' you ain't but one man. Even if you're tough, you won't stand no kind of chance goin' up ag'in them."

Adams heeled his mule forward, tugging the lead rope on

his pack animal. Slocum fell in beside him as they rode west at an easy gait.

One thought kept nagging Slocum. He'd shown Pearl his clip full of money, a stupid mistake because he'd trusted her apparent innocence, her shy manner. All of this was his fault and now he knew he'd been set up by Pearl, probably at Jake Willow's request after she'd told him about the gift he'd brought to Myra. It was an accident when she discovered he was also carrying that much money, and it only sweetened the pot.

Adams turned to him. "How'd these folks rob you?" he asked tonelessly, as if it didn't really matter to him.

"I played the part of a fool with a woman, a young girl. I thought she was interested in me, when all she was after was what I was carrying in my poke."

Adams grinned a toothless grin. "You won't be the first man who got took by a she-devil wearin' a skirt. I done it more'n my share of times."

"I should have known better. It was too easy."

"Said the same thing myself once or twice. I found there's two things a man had oughta be scared of. One's a feller who's crazy mean, like Cut Face Jake. The other's a woman with her eye out fer money."

"I'm not afraid of Willow. All I've gotta do is find him."

Adams gave him a curious stare. "You may come to regret them words, Slocum. Findin' him ain't gonna be the hard part. It's what happens when he finds *you* that you'd best be worryin' about."

6

"How far is it to this Crow's Nest?" Slocum asked, made edgy by the slow pace of Adams's mules. It was getting on toward noon, and the only living creatures they'd seen were deer and a few buffalo.

"We'll make it tomorrow sometime, if we don't run into trouble of some kind or 'nother."

"What kind of trouble?"

Adams shrugged, giving the countryside a careful examination. "This end of the Nations has got trouble of damn near every kind. Outlaws lookin' fer easy pickin's. Highwaymen who figure to rob a traveler who don't keep his eyes open fer an ambush. Renegade Injuns, mostly young bucks who jump the reservation to go on a horse-stealin' spree." He glanced at Slocum's bay. "That Remount stud will draw 'em like flies to buffalo droppings. A good horse is any Injun's most prized possession, an' most of 'em's got a good eye for horseflesh. You learn to ride real slow through these hills, an' pay attention to what's around you. There's renegades or drifters who'd kill me fer my bottles of whiskey. I've been robbed more'n once in this end of the Territory. Course, the western part is worse, on account it's

Comanche an' Kiowa land. They're the worst of the lot. A Comanche warrior is near 'bout the deadliest human bein' on earth an' they ain't scared of nothin'. That's how come Cut Face can run guns to 'em, 'cause nobody with a brain that ain't been pickled will enter Comanche land. Kiowa neither. Cut Face is just crazy enough to try it, an' 'cause he don't have the sense to act scared of 'em, they do business with him. A Comanche or a Kiowa respects men who don't show no fear. Jake Willow is too goddamn crazy to know he's supposed to be scared of anybody.''

Slocum recalled his scrapes with Comanches a few years ago, and he couldn't help but agree with Adams. ''A Comanche rides a horse like he was born on its back,'' Slocum said. ''Makes 'em real hard to hit with a rifle. A Kiowa is nearly as bad. But it don't matter to me whether Jake Willow is crazy or not. He was in cahoots with that girl and they took money that was mine, besides stealing a gift I brought down from Springfield to give to a pretty lady in Fort Smith.''

Adams watched the horizon. ''Is your money an' that gift worth dyin' for?'' he asked.

''I've put my life on the line for less,'' he replied as he took his own close look at their surroundings: empty forested hills and scattered open meadows with grass turning brown as fall ended the growing season.

Adams gave him a sideways glance. ''You're either tougher'n you look or lucky,'' he said, guiding his mules up a gentle rise to a ridge dotted with red oak and elm.

''Maybe a little of both,'' Slocum told the old man, which was the truth as he saw it. He would never have survived the war without a bit of luck.

''Couldn't help noticin' you carry your pistol backwards,'' Adams said. ''I reckon you got a reason.''

"It's faster. For me."

"Are you claimin' to be a pistoleer?"

"I'm not claiming to be anything besides a man who wants his stolen goods back."

"You're carryin' enough guns to start a war all by yourself, Slocum. I'm nearly sixty years old. Seen a lot of men with guns come an' go in my time. I've knowed a goodly share of hardcases too, men who don't need a passel of guns to make 'em dangerous. I can't quite figure out what it is that makes you so all-fired determined to square off ag'in a feller like Cut Face, even if it was fer all the money in the world."

"It's really simple enough. It sticks in my craw like sand when somebody steals from me. I aim to teach Jake Willow and his girlfriend a lesson about owning money and property." He listened to the creak of saddle leather while Adams considered what he'd told him.

"There's some men can't be taught no lessons," Adams said after a bit. "They only learn the hard way."

Slocum thought about it. "Then I'll put a bullet through him and that'll be the end of it. He'll learn the hard way, only he won't live long enough to profit by it."

The old man chuckled again. "I sure as hell hope you're as tough as you sound, John Slocum. If you ain't, somebody'll be diggin' a six-foot hole for you in Injun Territory before too awful long."

Dusk came early to the plains and hills around them as the days got shorter with the change of seasons. They'd ridden all day without seeing another soul. Once, Slocum thought he saw a thin column of smoke rise into a late-day sky many miles to the west, but with the winds stirring he couldn't be sure.

Adams remained silent most of the afternoon, his eyes roaming back and forth, and it appeared he was wary now, more cautious than ever. Slocum could almost feel the old man's tension as they rode deeper into Indian country.

Lengthening shadows fell away from trees and brush with the arrival of sunset. And as darkness came, the winds died down to gentler breezes.

"How much farther is it?" Slocum asked.

"Maybe four or five miles. From here on we gotta be careful an' stay hid in them trees wherever we can. My ol' nose don't hardly ever fail me, an' fer the last couple of hours I've been smelling Injuns. Wood smoke travels fer miles on a wind, you know, an' I sure as hell been smellin' smoke. Could be it's a renegade camp, or maybe just one campfire in front of us someplace."

Slocum pulled his Winchester from its saddle boot and sent a load into the firing chamber with the lever. He lowered the hammer gently and booted the long gun again. "Just in case we strike a camp that ain't friendly," he explained when Adams gave him a look.

"Won't hardly find no friendly camps out here," Adams said in a quiet voice.

They rode into a grassy arroyo and suddenly Adams raised his hand, calling a halt. "Smell that smoke?" he asked. "It ain't far from here, whoever it is."

Now Slocum also scented smoke on the wind. "Just over that next rise maybe," he replied.

"That's the way I got it figured," Adams said. "If we was real smart we'd ride around it."

"It could be Jake Willow and the woman," Slocum said. "If it is, we'll settle accounts right here and now, before he gets to the Crow's Nest."

"You'll have to be part Injun to slip up close enough to find out," Adams warned.

Slocum halted his stud and swung down from the saddle, handing Adams his reins. "My ma never told me if there was any Indian blood in my veins, but I'll be back," he promised, taking his rifle from the boot. "Give me a quarter hour to slip over that hilltop."

Adams sounded doubtful. "If'n you ain't back in half an hour I'm keeping this bay fer myself. You won't need it where you're goin', if it's Cut Face camped beyond that ridge."

Slocum understood the old man's worries. "Just wait here for fifteen minutes."

"I'm keepin' the bay stud if you ain't back," Adams reminded him.

"It's okay, but make damn sure you wait that quarter hour or I'll come looking for you."

Adams chuckled softly. "You ain't got much choice but to trust me, Slocum, if you're dead set on seein' what's on the far side of that ridge. We ain't been acquainted but a day. How come you'd be so sure I'll be here?"

"I'm a pretty good judge of men, and I know what would happen to you if you took my horse. I spent a lot of time among the Pawnee and Cheyenne. A fair amount scouting for Apaches in Arizona Territory. I know how to kill a man so he's real sorry he double-crossed me."

"Them's Cheyenne leggin's you're wearin'. I saw that right off, so I'm inclined to believe you. But the owlhoot you're after, Jake Willow, is as good as any full-blood at killin' folks. You make sure you give it some thought before you brace him . . . if it's him across them hills yonder."

"I don't need to think about it," Slocum replied, taking a deep breath of cool air, drawing in the scent of smoke.

"When I set out to settle a score my mind's made up to settle it. If that fire belongs to Willow, he's gonna regret the day he threw in with the woman to rob me."

He crept forward on the balls of his feet, clutching the Winchester to his chest.

Off in the dusky dark a nighthawk screeched, its warning call to its prey. Slocum felt a bit like prey at this moment as he walked quietly toward the smell from a campfire.

Once, he glanced over his shoulder to watch Adams move toward a line of red oaks. If Adams had in mind stealing his horse, there would be another day of reckoning not too far in the future.

Prairie grasses swished across his moccasins, a whispering noise he couldn't avoid where grass was deep. He moved as quickly as he could down the arroyo, then began climbing a gentle slope toward the crest of a row of thickly wooded hills. As he moved closer the odor of smoke grew stronger, filling his nostrils with acrid scent.

"Maybe I got lucky," he whispered, hunkering down to make as small a target as possible until he reached the first thickets of oak.

Stepping softly between tree trunks, Slocum remembered an assualt on Union lines at Franklin, Tennessee. After the bitter fighting at Gettysburg he'd thought nothing could equal the bloodshed and death he'd seen there. But at Franklin, in what was a senseless charge by outnumbered Confederate forces under the command of General John Bell Hood, an even more terrible fate awaited Southern soldiers. Over eight thousand men in gray would die that day in Tennessee, those Tennessee hills covered with bullet-torn bodies. Slocum knew nothing could be worse than what they'd endured that day. The battle at Franklin was where a lot of young boys became men.

Closer to the top of the ridge, he slowed his cautious footsteps until he was down to a crawl, weaving back and forth among oak trunks, pausing behind one, then another, listening for the slightest sound, watching the dark for any sign of movement among forest shadows.

"Not much farther." He mouthed the words without saying them out loud. A faint ringing began in his ears, and he could hear his heartbeat in the silence around him.

Off to his left a cricket started to chirp. Again, further away this time, he heard the hunting call of a nighthawk as it soared across inky skies.

A few feet at a time, he reached the ridge and peered over the rim carefully. Down below he saw the glimmer of a fire, a tiny speck of light in a blanket of darkness beaming from the bottom of a dry streambed.

Squatting on his haunches, he scanned the circle of light around the flames. He counted five, then six figures sitting near the fire, and even from a distance of several hundred yards he could make them out as Indians.

"It ain't Jake Willow," he whispered to himself, relaxing his grip on the stock of the rifle. He told himself the Indians were most likely a hunting party . . . harmless unless they were provoked.

He inched backward until he could stand, beginning a slow return downhill, still cautious, moving from tree trunk to tree trunk where shadows were the deepest.

Slocum crossed the arroyo balancing the Winchester in his hand, heading for the spot where he'd left Adams. This wasn't what he'd had in mind when he rode out of Springfield last week, merely looking forward to delivering a present to a beautiful lady. Events had turned around on him in one hell of a hurry, and that didn't suit him.

He found Adams and his horse waiting in a grove of trees

not far from the grassy bottom of the ravine.

"Who was it?" Adams asked in a low voice.

"Six Indian bucks. Looked to me like a hunting party camped for the night."

"Maybe," Adams said as Slocum booted his rifle and mounted his horse.

"What the hell does that mean?" Slocum asked, gathering his reins to ride off.

"Depends on what they's huntin', Slocum. Could be they's friends of Cut Face Jake, sent out to make sure he wasn't bein' followed."

7

They broke a cold camp at dawn, spending a chilly night in a grove of red oak beside a clear-running stream, taking turns at standing watch huddled inside blankets since it was too risky for a fire. The smell of smoke might draw Indians the same way it had warned Slocum and Adams of the Indian campsite. Adams hadn't said much during the night, but as they chewed jerky at dawn he brought up the subject of Jake Willow again.

"Must be a powerful lot of money Cut Face stole from you to make you willin' to take a chance like this. Most of the regulars hangin' around the Crow's Nest know me, so they ain't gonna get jumpy when I ride in. But you're a stranger, an' you could be the law, so you can count on bein' looked at real close."

"It's a sizable amount, what they took from me," Slocum said as he watched a brightening eastern horizon. "As to the part about being looked at, I've been through it before. The only worry I've got is when the girl sees me. She'll tell Willow who I am, if he don't know already, and Willow will know I've come for my money and valuables. If there's to be any shooting, it'll happen then."

"Cut Face'll be sided by a few of his friends. Some is renegade Injuns. A couple are wanted men up in Kansas Territory where Cut Face used to hang his hat. He got cross-ways with one of the Earps—Wyatt, I b'lieve it was—an' he cleared out of that country a couple years back. He's a tough son of a bitch, but he ain't stupid."

Slocum knew the Earp brothers. While they had mean reputations as lawmen, normally they were affable enough. Railhead towns in Kansas required tough peace officers. James Hickok was just as fearless, although even Hickok himself didn't know where the nickname "Wild Bill" came from. Someone had told Slocum it was a mistake made by a reporter from back East, perhaps intentionally, to help sell fanciful tales about Hickok's exploits, that Hickok's reputation was based on half-truths, like that of a number of notable figures in the West. Slocum only knew of one man who was every bit as mean as his reputation. John Wesley Hardin was a true gunfighter, a remorseless killer who killed for some dark pleasure he found in it. Not many years ago Hardin and Hickok had faced each other in Abilene, according to a story Slocum had heard from a friend who was there. Neither Hardin nor Hickok would draw against each other, and it was still the subject of debate as to whether it was out of respect or fear.

"I reckon I'll have to take things the way they come," Slocum told Adams. "One thing's for damn sure. I'll be asking for my money back one way or another."

The sun came over hills behind them while they headed west, toward a place near a village called Talequah where John Slocum meant to make an appointment with Cut Face Jake Willow and a girl who'd made a fool out of him. She'd been one hell of a good ride on a bucking mattress, but not good enough to be worth a thousand dollars.

"Here's where you an' me part company," Adams said, sitting his mule inside a grove of trees on a knob above a shallow valley. In the distance, they could see columns of smoke rising.

"I understand," Slocum replied. "I've got a favor to ask, although you don't owe me one. If you run across Willow, or see this slender blond girl down yonder, I'd be obliged if you didn't mention seeing me to either one of 'em. I'll have to find a way to brace Willow when he isn't surrounded by his pardners, if I can."

"I won't say nothin'," Adams promised, giving the Crow's Nest a squint in the sun's early glare. "I got no use fer Cut Face myself anyways. He'd as soon cut my throat as look at me, an' I'm smart enough to know it. But I'm gonna give you one last warnin', Slocum. Think about it real hard afore you jump Cut Face fer your money. Don't matter how much it was. A dead man can't spend money, an' you can always make some more. Remember that Jake won't fight you fair. He'll slip up on your backside, or shoot you from ambush, maybe cut your throat whilst you're asleep. He ain't got no honor 'bout him." Adams turned to Slocum and grinned. "I been wonderin' 'bout somethin', an' you sure as hell don't got to answer no questions from me."

"What's that?" Slocum asked, studying the best approach to the Crow's Nest so he wouldn't be seen.

Now Adams chuckled. "Was wonderin' if maybe the woman is what you're really after. Some men has got a jealous side, an' if she run off with Cut Face it'd be understandable, I reckon, fer a man to want the woman back."

"It isn't the woman," he answered.

Adams collected his reins to ride off the knob. "A man

like me ain't got no use fer a woman in the first place.
They's nothin' but trouble, if you ask me. It all started with
ol' Adam an' Eve, you know. They was happy in that gar-
den, till the bitch made him take a bite of just one apple.
Ever since, we've been cast out of all the better places.
That's how we ended up here, watchin' out fer Injuns an'
backshooters an' flooded rivers an' rattlesnakes, the two-
legged variety an' the ones that crawl. It don't surprise me
none that a woman was in cahoots with Cut Face takin' your
money. Damn near all the females I've knowed is worse'n
rattlesnakes. At least a rattler gives a man a warnin' before
it strikes.''

"Women can be a comfort in bed," Slocum said, turning
his stud to ride south, planning to skirt the Crow's Nest first
to get the lay of things. "I'm grateful for you showing me
where this place is. Maybe we'll meet up someplace again
on a trail to another town. Ride careful, Adams.''

"You too, Slocum, an' remember what I said. Watch your
back an' sleep with one eye open.''

Slocum waved and heeled his horse south, keeping to the
trees wherever he could, hoping Adams was a man of his
word. If Adams told Willow someone was on his trail, Willow would come looking for him with his partners siding
him, making it sure to be one hell of a one-sided fight.

The Crow's Nest was a single log building nestled in a tiny
meadow. Several big tents had been erected across a creek
from the trading post. Stacks of cured buffalo hides lay all
over the clearing. A few pole corrals held more than a dozen
horses and mules. Men were about, three or four, washing
clothes in the stream or taking baths themselves. Three Indians with long braided hair lounged on the narrow front
porch of the trading post. Slocum saw all of this from a

thickly wooded hilltop south of the settlement, approaching as close as he dared on foot after leaving the stud tied in a ravine behind him. For a time he simply watched what was happening, thinking things through, figuring out how he'd slip down to the store without being noticed.

What he saw confounded him a little. There were so few men there, it hardly looked like the outlaw roost Adams claimed it was. The men he could see looked like fur trappers or hide hunters. Only one man carried a gun that he could see from a distance.

"Something don't add up," he said to himself as Ben Adams rode slowly into the settlement leading his pack mule. "If this is a place for bad men, they sure as hell aren't showing themselves now, and they let Adams ride in like he owned the place."

He watched Adams swing down in front of the store. One of the Indians began talking to Adams, using hand sign as well as words, and a few times he pointed north, gesturing.

"Something's happened," Slocum whispered. "I'd bet money Jake Willow and the girl aren't there . . . if I had money to make a bet."

A few moments later Adams looked up at the hills where Slocum was hidden. Adams knew which direction Slocum had ridden when they parted company. Was Adams trying to tell him all was clear? That Willow and the girl weren't there?

It would be risky as hell riding down to find out if Adams had news of Willow's whereabouts. But Slocum had been taking big risks all his life, it seemed, and his patience was wearing thin right about now.

When he saw Adams tie his mules to a hitching post, Slocum made up his mind. Inching backward, he wheeled and went for his horse. The Crow's Nest looked almost de-

serted, half of its sagging army field tents vacant. For a so-
called outlaw hideout it was too quiet, too peaceful, as if
something had occurred causing men wanted by the law to
pull out for reasons only Adams could explain now that he'd
talked to the Indian.

Slocum mounted his bay and readied his guns, taking a
hammer thong off his Colt .44 and pulling his Winchester
a little higher for an easier pull. He hung his shotgun from
the saddlehorn by its shoulder strap, after checking to make
sure both barrels had loads.

Winding through the woods, picking his way, he rode out
on a hilltop above the Crow's Nest and sat in plain sight
for a time, finding Adams still talking to one of the Indians.

The Indian saw him first, pointing to the hill. Adams
made a turn, shading his eyes from the sun, eyes that he'd
admitted were bad. Then he made a motion, beckoning Slocum to ride down to the trading post.

"I guessed right," Slocum said with a sigh, urging his
horse downslope at an easy walk. "Jake Willow and the girl
ain't here. For some reason or other they cleared out just
ahead of us . . . if this is where they were headed in the first
place."

Several curious hide hunters stopped what they were doing at the stream to watch his approach, but not one made
any sort of move toward a gun. Adams started walking toward him before he reached the creek. As Slocum rode
across water only a foot deep in the deepest spots, Adams
stopped and waited for him.

"They's gone," Adams said when he rode up and halted
his bay. "There was a hell of a ruckus here yesterday, an'
Cut Face got word of it just in time. Six U.S. marshals rode
in with guns drawn. Had the place surrounded, that Injun
over yonder told me just now. They arrested four men.

Hauled 'em off wearin' iron bracelets. Said they was takin' 'em to Fort Smith.''

"Judge Parker's deputies," Slocum told him, giving the store and tents a second examination. "I saw them ride out the night I was robbed. Looks like they found the Crow's Nest without too much trouble." He gazed down at Adams again. "Any word on where Jake Willow and the woman went?''

Adams nodded. "Ol' Four Feathers over yonder said Cut Face saw what was happenin' when they arrested Spikes an' his three sons. Cut Face slipped down here that night. He got that Injun to buy him some supplies fer the trail. Said he was headed up to Kansas where he's got friends an' places to hide till things cool off fer him down here. Four Feathers said Jake was carryin' a big roll of money, like maybe he'd robbed a bank somewheres.''

"It was me he robbed," Slocum reminded him, thinking of the long trail up to the Kansas line. "Was the girl with him?''

"Four Feathers said he didn't see no woman, but Jake made it sound like he weren't goin' up yonder by hisself. Jake's renegade pardners was off lookin' fer cattle to steal, the Injun said when I asked him. They was lucky too, 'pears like.''

Slocum let his shoulders sag. He faced many long days in the seat of a saddle. "I'm going after Willow. If I can pick up their tracks it'll make it a hell of a lot easier. Maybe I can catch up before they get to Wichita or Newton. Thanks for all your help, Adams. I still owe you a debt.''

"All I ask is that you forgit where you heard this," Adams replied. "If Cut Face finds out I put you on his trail, he'll come after me like stink comes right behind shit. He'll kill me deader'n a fence post.''

"Not if I find him first," Slocum promised, clenching his teeth in anger when he thought about what lay in store. "Thanks again," he added, sending his bay northward, toward the Kansas line, several hard days' ride away.

"Best of luck," Adams said to his back as he rode across the clearing away from the Crow's Nest. "I got this feelin' down in my gut you're gonna need it."

Slocum did not look back, thinking of nothing but his quarry now as he headed the big Thoroughbred up a gentle slope.

"If I can only find their goddamn tracks," he muttered, making a study of the ground when he came to open places where two horses would leave traces of their passing, perhaps only to an experienced eye.

When he crested a heavily wooded ridge he began riding in widening circles, his head bent down, eyes sweeping grassy spots and barren soil for the slightest impression made by a hoof. He understood how much patience was required to find tracks made by a cautious rider, and forced himself to ride slowly, missing nothing as he circled farther north.

As he rode he considered the bitter twist of fate that had brought him here when he'd intended to ride back to Colorado with his money. He'd only agreed to make a slight detour from the route he'd planned to deliver the dagger to Myra. And now it seemed everything had backfired on him, all because of his carelessness and a woman.

"Adams may be right," he said under his breath, reining the stud across a clearing. "Some women can be every damn bit as dangerous as a rattler . . . but I sure as hell would hate to think of bein' too long without one."

In the middle of the clearing he suddenly halted the bay and swung down, kneeling, tracing his fingertips gently over a slight scratch on a stretch of flat rock. His eyes roamed back and forth until he found another impression, hardly more than a thin line made by an iron horseshoe on a slab of stone.

"Two horses!" he said savagely, standing up, gazing in the direction indicated by the prints. Slocum's eyes narrowed. "I'm right behind you now, Jake, you and your pretty lady. You ain't got it figured out yet, but the two of you just bought yourselves into a hell of a lot more trouble than you bargained for."

8

A time or two he lost the tracks, forcing him back in a wide circle until he found them again. As the sun rose toward midday, he relaxed somewhat, still angry, but resigned to a slow, dogged pursuit until his Thoroughbred's longer strides and stamina brought him closer to Willow and Pearl. When he found a clean print and examined the edges for sharpness, he judged the tracks were a half a day old. And as he rode over a broad expanse of gently rolling hills, he considered how much more difficult his task might have been were it not for a chance meeting with Ben Adams, and his somewhat reluctant cooperation. Adams and the others he'd talked to seemed to genuinely fear Jake Willow, and now Slocum began to wonder just how difficult it would be to take him down—he wouldn't give up the money or the dagger willingly—and how great his own chances were of riding into a bushwhacking somewhere along the trail to Kansas.

Later, Slocum ended his deliberations with a grunt. "If he tries to jump me, it'll only get it over sooner." He glanced at forests and possible hiding places around him, cords of muscle standing out in his neck when he gritted his teeth. "Make your move, Cut Face," he snarled. "Let's see if you're as goddamn good as they say you are." Slocum trusted his senses to warn him in the nick of time.

A flock of blackbirds rose suddenly from a swale not far to the north. He knew something had driven them into the sky, something they feared, a presence in the forest that did not belong.

Slocum halted the stud and drew his rifle, watching the birds and the direction they flew. Sweeping off to the east, eight or nine blackbirds winged rapidly along the current of a prevailing wind, darting among treetops as if they sensed danger.

"It could be a big cat," he said aloud. "Or a man who headed back down the tracks he made to see if he's being followed."

He urged his bay into a dense stand of thicker oaks where leafy branches cast shadows on the forest floor, making him harder to see, hiding the outline of rider and horse should a rifleman be waiting in ambush where the birds had departed so suddenly. His bay was not a range-bred animal, and Slocum couldn't trust its senses the way he might a Palouse pony, or a mustang. And as he neared the top of a hill, he knew his horse's hooves made too much noise in fallen leaves littering the ground. So he stopped, swinging down, deciding to go the rest of the way on foot until he was certain no danger lay ahead.

He tied the stud to a low limb and crept forward, his rifle at the ready against his right shoulder, moving quietly in moccasins, scarcely making a sound. If Jake Willow had set a trap for him beyond the next rise, these silent hills would soon resound with gunfire.

"All this," he muttered, inching closer, "because of a

damn blond-haired girl and a stiff prick." He was a thousand dollars poorer and missing an expensive antique dagger that had been entrusted to him, all on account of Pearl and his weakness for beautiful women.

Crouching down, he edged over to a stout tree trunk with a view of the ravine beyond. Peering carefully around the oak, he saw a shallow, treeless basin overgrown with yellowed buffalo grass, a narrow stream coursing through it. Where the stream came from the forest roughly a quarter mile to the west, a lone buffalo bull, shaggy in its growing winter coat, drank from the water's edge. The old bull had numerous scars on its hindquarters and flank. It had probably been driven from a herd by a younger bull when it could no longer defend itself or the cows it claimed for raising young.

Slocum lowered his rifle. All his caution approaching the hilltop had been a waste of valuable time, yet it was far wiser to be cautious than dead from a bushwhacker's bullet.

He turned back for his horse, determined somehow to make up the time he'd lost.

Another cold night camp left him restless, angry, yet he had no choice but to give the stud time to graze and rest. A horse with an empty belly, no matter what its breeding, had no stamina or reserves for speed. Thus Slocum sat at the base of a tree in the dark nursing a bottle of whiskey, which was reasonably good for a brand found in a frontier town like Fort Smith. He chewed jerky under a clear sky illuminated by winking stars and a slice of the new moon. He'd spent countless nights like this, alone on some dark prairie, and while most times he felt content with the serenity, tonight he harbored too many thoughts of revenge to enjoy his peaceful surroundings. Resting his head against the tree, he allowed his mind to wander. Random thoughts, old memories, drifted through his brain. Passing time, he remembered the girl he'd met during his stay in Springfield, a stunning redhead with lips so full she seemed to wear a continual pouting expression.

Her aloof demeanor was the first thing to attract his notice when they were introduced. Her name was Sara Jane.

"Why are you staring at my bosom, Mr. Slocum? Bradford said you were a true gentleman, a man of refinement." Her silky voice stirred him.

"I'm sorry, Miss Conner. Please do accept my apology, for I take some pride in the use of proper manners. I can only offer a weak excuse for my stare. Your lovely gown is designed to reveal an inordinate amount of your beautiful chest. In Denver, at the nicer places I frequent, women seem less inclined to wear dresses so fashionable. The latest fashions come more slowly to western territories like Colorado. Your gown must have been very expensive to be so tastefully tailored."

She smiled. "I suppose I was given the wrong impression by the direction your eyes took momentarily. I accept your apology and your kind offer of a glass of sherry."

He summoned a bartender to their table. The Crystal Palace was certainly one of Springfield's finer establishments, with elegant upholstered chairs and polished mahogany tables, a quiet place for people with money and breeding, according to Bradford Thomas. He'd introduced Sara Jane to Slocum, departing after their sumptuous dinner of steak and potatoes followed by slices of rum pie. Now the barman arrived, dressed in a coat and string tie.

"Bring the lady a glass of your best sherry, and a snifter of brandy for myself," he said.

Sara Jane was watching him. "Bradford tells me you deal in blooded racehorses. He speaks very highly of you."

"We've known each other for some time. I've sold him a number of quality animals at a fair price." He was helpless to keep his eyes from straying down again to the cleavage between her ample breasts; lightly freckled, firm, spilling over the hem at the top of her dress, quivering slightly when she moved, as if girded too firmly in place by her bodice. "If I may be so bold, Miss Conner, you are truly one of the most beautiful women I've ever seen. You must have dozens of suitors."

She smiled again. "I'm very discriminating, if I may say so politely without sounding coy."

"As you can well afford to be. I'm honored that you would agree to remain and share a drink with me."

"You continue to stare at my bosom. Should I take it as a compliment as well?"

"Of course, although it may seem brash. I don't seem to be able to help myself."

Their drinks arrived, long-stemmed crystal goblets of sherry and brandy. As soon as the bartender left, Sara Jane raised her glass to her lips and hesitated before she drank. "Then I must assume you're wondering what my breasts look like when I take off my clothing, Mr. Slocum. What other conclusion can I draw from your behavior?"

"I suppose I am, even though it may not be gentlemanly of me to admit it."

She took a sip of her drink, moistening her lips with the tip of her tongue after she swallowed. "There are two kinds of gentlemen, in my experience," she said quietly. "One is a public performer with well-practiced manners."

"And the other?" Slocum asked, noticing a very slight reddening in her cheeks.

She glanced around them to see if anyone was listening. "I have known perfect gentlemen in a bedroom, Mr. Slocum. These are quite rare types, men who know how to treat a lady in bed, if you know what I imply."

"I'm quite sure I understand, and in all modesty I truly believe I am one of those gentlemen who shows only the greatest concern for a woman's comfort and pleasure while sharing her bed and her charms."

"Is that so?" Sara Jane asked, arching one eyebrow, a slow grin widening her lush lips. "Then perhaps later I'll give you the opportunity to demonstrate this concern for my comfort and pleasure, after we've had our drinks. If you'll promise me to remember I am a woman who must be treated gently."

He nodded and tipped up his goblet, draining it, ordering another by holding his empty glass aloft when the barman looked their way. "You have my word on it," he said.

"Harder!" she cried, screwing her eyelids tightly shut as he drove his cock into her hungry wet cunt. "Hurt me, John! Give me all of it! Please!"

He drove every inch of his long thick shaft inside her and felt her stiffen, her fingernails clawing his shoulders until he felt them draw blood.

"Pinch my nipple! Do it hard!" Sara Jane gasped, throwing her silken mound against the base of his blood-engorged prick as bedsprings creaked with their frenzied lovemaking, her moans and cries filling her bedroom with added sounds of passion.

He squeezed her right nipple between his thumb and forefinger, increasing the pressure while she rocked and hunched atop the mattress.

"Oh, yes, John!" she squealed, reaching a climax so

quickly he wasn't fully prepared for the power of her twisting muscles or the hammering thrusts of her abdomen.

She became completely rigid underneath him, straining, her fingers like iron clamping his back. She drew in a breath and held it, her lips parted, teeth clenched at the height of her ecstasy.

Slocum felt his testicles rise, although he hadn't had time to come close to his own orgasm. Still thrusting despite the grip of her legs around him, he pushed his prick in and out of her slippery cunt, her juices dribbling down on his balls and inner thighs.

Sara Jane exhaled, a mighty rush of air, collapsing on the damp sheet as limply as a rag doll. "I can't . . . take any . . . more," she gasped.

He ignored her feeble protest, driving harder, faster as he neared his release, sure in the knowledge he could arouse her again when the motion of his rock-hard cock reawakened the fires within her.

"Please. No more," she whimpered softly.

"I'm almost there," he grunted, panting for wind.

"Why won't you stop?" she asked hoarsely, her arms lying at her sides. "You're hurting me. . . ."

A warm sensation grew stronger in his groin, moving down his thighs, upward across his belly, and he knew he couldn't stop now, not until his seed was spent.

"You . . . promised to treat me . . . gently," she continued, but as she said it she lifted her hands to his neck, curling her fingers into the coal-black hair touching his shoulders.

Again he was silent, poking his shaft all the way to the hilt between the moist lips at the tops of her legs.

Slowly at first, Sara Jane began to rock gently on the bed in time with his rhythm. Her calves tightened behind his knees while her heels dug into the mattress for a purchase.

His thrusts became a furious series of stabbing blows into her cunt—he grabbed brass rods in the headboard of her bed to hold himself in position.

"Oh, John," she sighed as her love fever returned. She put her lips to his cheek, sucking his skin with wet kisses while her body trembled with desire.

Slocum was near complete exhaustion when his balls exploded with tremendous intensity, sending a fountain of jism inside her in regular spurts.

"Not yet!" she cried, bowing her spine, thrusting to meet him.

He continued to hammer the depths of her pussy until she reached another orgasm, weaker than the first, less intense but with genuine vigor. She stiffened again and groaned, shaking from head to toe, until she fell flat on the bed, utterly spent, gasping for air.

He lay quietly between her legs for several minutes while his own breathing slowed. She lay beneath him, motionless with her eyes closed.

"You do know how to treat a lady," she whispered near his ear.

"I always make every attempt to be a man of my word," he told her.

"You also have the biggest cock I've ever seen," she added with a smile. "It's like a tree trunk, and best of all, you do know how to use it."

He couldn't remember hearing any complaints, although he did not say this to Sara Jane Conner that night.

9

He removed the bay's hobbles at dawn and saddled for another long day aboard the horse. Such was the nature of manhunting, and he knew its hardships well. When he was mounted, he found tracks without too much difficulty despite slanted sunlight, and set out to follow them.

Willow and the girl were moving unerringly northwest with less regard for hiding their tracks, and in places their horses' prints were widely spaced, deeper at the toe, proof of greater haste than before.

"Cut Face is probably in a hurry to get to Kansas so he can start spending my money," Slocum muttered. If Willow cut one of the big cattle trails he would follow it, making it virtually impossible to find his tracks amid the cloven-hoofed prints made by thousands of longhorns. Then it would be guesswork as to the direction he and Pearl took, although they would most likely go to the first of the larger cow towns along the Chisholm. Slocum recalled a place named Coffeyville just across the Kansas line, large enough to have a bank that was frequently robbed and several saloons. But if Jake Willow wanted to spend Slocum's money and sell the stolen dagger, he needed a place the size of

Wichita or Abilene, towns served by a railroad. The girl might even beg him into riding a train up to Kansas City, where the finer things could be bought with John Slocum's money.

And the longer he thought about it the madder Slocum got, until by mid-morning he was in a rage all over again, his teeth gritted, jaw muscles working when he was unable to push what had happened to him from his mind.

"I may give up women entirely," he told the horse. "Look at what the last one's cost me."

The bay's ears turned backward at the sound of his voice and just for a moment, Slocum wished his horse could talk.

Coffeyville lay on a flat plain just beyond a wood stake for a boundary marker that told him he was in Kansas Territory now. He reined in near the outskirts of town to look things over, watching everyone moving about, paying particular attention to any horses with a golden buckskin coloring. It had been years since he'd last visited Coffeyville, and he was somewhat surprised to find bank buildings made of brick along the city's main street. A sign above one bank read "Condon & Company," while another proclaimed it was the "First National Bank," a two-story affair with an odd pointed roofline that could be seen for miles. And not to his surprise, the balance of the town seemed to consist of saloons and general stores, all meant to provide what hungry and thirsty travelers needed, since Coffeyville was hardly a place where a great number of people settled permanently.

"Looks quiet enough," he said to himself as he urged his bay forward again. Slocum's first order of business was to inform the local law of the reason for his visit, in case gunplay started between himself and Willow. And there was a chance Jake Willow was known in these parts. Perhaps a peace officer had seen him ride into town.

He approached Coffeyville from a back side, avoiding the main road into town from the south with a very real purpose, to look over the horses boarded at the town's livery, checking for any dun-colored animals that could belong to Jake. Slocum rode up to a set of corrals behind the stable and passed a glance over every horse, finding a buckskin gelding with a Circle Y brand on its flank and recent sweat stains from a saddle.

"That'll be his horse," Slocum told himself, swinging down. He could inquire with the liveryman as to the yellow horse's ownership.

He tied the stud to a fence rail and walked around the corrals toward the front of the barn, examining the backs of every building fronting Main Street to see if anyone had noticed his arrival. But for the most part the citizens of Coffeyville were out and about on personal business and no one seemed to be paying any attention to him.

Slocum found an old man in faded overalls forking hay into one of the horse pens.

"Howdy, mister," Slocum began, ambling up to the fence. "I was curious about that buckskin gelding back yonder. Is it for sale at a reasonable price?"

"I jest bought it last night," the liveryman said, working a chaw of tobacco into the other cheek. "Bought him from this halfbreed who claimed he was a hell of a solid trail horse. He's a bit on the thin side."

"Did the man who sold him to you have a scar on his face?" Slocum asked.

"How come yer wantin' to know?" the stableman asked with a sudden look of worry crossing his face. "Are you sayin' that buckskin was stole or somethin'?"

"I'm not saying anything of the kind, mister. Just wondering if I knew the owner, is all."

The old man appeared to relax somewhat. "If you know that horse, then you know who owned him. It was Cut Face Jake Willow who sold him to me, him an' that chestnut mare in the corral back yonder with him."

"Then the chestnut belonged to a blond girl. Her name is Pearl."

The liveryman nodded, giving Slocum a quizzical eye. "You seem to know a lot about 'em, stranger, fer a man who started out askin' fer a price on the horse."

"I'm looking for Willow and the woman."

The man's eyes fell to Slocum's gun. "If'n I was you I'd be real careful askin' questions 'bout Jake. If you know anythin' at all 'bout him, you know to be careful 'round him."

"Is he still in town?"

"Nope. I traded him two fresh horses fer them two they was ridin' an' they lit out of here like their tail feathers was on fire. That was last night. Seems I remember they stopped off at Bob Miller's store like they aimed to buy supplies."

"Did you happen to see which way they rode out of town?" he asked.

"No, sir, I didn't, an' even if I did I wouldn't be inclined to mention it. If Cut Face ever found out I put a man on his trail, he'd come back an' kill me fer sure. You ain't said so, but you sure as hell got the look of a lawman about you, an' ol' Jake's had a few troubles with the law, so I hear."

"I'm not the law," Slocum protested. "Willow stole something from me and I want it back."

At that, the old man grinned. "I bet it was that pretty gal he had with him. She was cute, in a plain sorta way. By the looks of their horses, they'd come a considerable distance to get here."

"It isn't the girl. I'd be mighty grateful if you could tell me which direction they went."

"Can't say fer sure, mister. But you could ask Bob Miller if Willow told him where they was goin'. I'd nearly swear they rode the west fork of that road yonder, which would take 'em up to Wichita. But they coulda rode north across the Fall River. I wasn't payin' no attention. On purpose. There's times when it ain't healthy to know some things."

"I understand," Slocum said with a sigh. "I'll ask over at the store. Much obliged for the information. You might help me just a bit if you told me what color horses they traded for, so I'd know from a distance if I'm following the right pair."

"That'd be easy. Don't see no harm in tellin' you that much either. Cut Face is ridin' a big black geldin'. The girl is on a sorrel with two hind socks. Both good horses too. Not a lame bone in either one of·'em. Jake knows a bit 'bout horses an' he picked out good distance-ridin' stock, the kind that can cover some ground."

Slocum tipped his hat to the liveryman and walked back to the rear of the place to mount his bay. From the information he'd gotten from the stable owner, he was at least ten or twelve hours behind Jake and the girl. He'd lost some time having to stop so often to look for their tracks. If he could be certain of Willow's destination he could ask the bay stud for speed, shortening the gap between him and his quarry.

Bob Miller introduced himself as soon as Slocum walked in the store. "What can I do for you, mister?"

"I'm afraid all I'm after right now is information. I was

told a man with a scar on his face came in your store last night to buy supplies. His name's Jake Willow, and he had a young girl with him.''

Miller's expectant smile vanished. ''I know him,'' Miller said. ''Can't say as it's no pleasure. Everybody in these parts knows Jake, an' he did have this girl with him. He bought a lot of whiskey an' ammunition. Some food, an' a pistol for the girl too. She wanted licorice whips an' peppermint sticks. Kinda odd combination, if you ask me, all them sweets an' a gun besides. I sold 'em a box of cartridges for the revolver.''

''Did they happen to mention where they were going, or ask for directions?''

Miller chuckled. ''Jake don't need no directions in this neck of the woods. I 'spect he knows every back trail all the way to Kansas City. Just bein' curious, but are you a U.S. marshal or somethin'?''

''I'm not a peace officer. Jake robbed me, and I intend to get my money back.''

''You'll need more'n luck, stranger, if you find him in the first place. There've been all sorts of rumors about how many men he's killed, an' hardly any of 'em was face-to-face, so I hear tell.''

Slocum turned to a store window. ''It would sure be a big help if I knew which direction they went.''

The storekeeper fiddled with his apron strings a moment. ''I did overhear the girl say somethin' about Kansas City, seein' all the sights, that sort of thing.''

''Then they're headed north?'' Slocum suggested.

''That'd be my guess. They'll have to cross the Neosho to get to Uniontown outside of Fort Scott. A man like Jake won't be too awful close to no army post, I don't reckon.''

Slocum started for the door. "I'm much obliged for what you told me," he said on his way out.

"Just be sure you forget where you heard it if you catch up to Jake," Miller said.

Slocum swung up on his bay, sighting north as a brisk fall wind lifted dust from the Kansas prairies. He remembered a plain devoid of any trees north of Coffeyville, which would make it harder for a man to hide out in the open. With a good horse under him he could make up for lost time. The chase was about to come down to a test of horseflesh.

He reined away from the hitch rail and struck a short lope out of town, tugging his hat down over his eyes to keep a stiff wind from blowing it off. The country he was about to cross was also very dry this late in the year, making it harder to find water for men and animals ... unless you knew where to look. And the land was hard, flinty rock, tough on a horse's hooves unless they were properly shod.

He rode out of Coffeyville at a steady gallop with the sun almost directly overhead. Fort Scott lay a day's ride to the north; thus it would be noon tomorrow before he struck Unionville and had a chance to buy a meager ration of supplies in case the trail took him to Kansas City. Slocum kept a five-dollar gold piece hidden in his boot lining, a habit from harder times when money, even a small amount, might be enough to keep him alive. For now he had ample foodstuffs and a bottle of whiskey. It was sufficient to keep him on the move without resorting to living off the land, hunting wild game.

"Water's gonna be the problem," he told himself, slowing his bay to a ground-eating trot. The stud could hold a steady trot all day without tiring, unless Lady Luck dealt him a bad hand—a stone bruise from a sharp piece of flint in the frog of the bay's foot, or a loose horseshoe.

Gritty dust blew in his eyes, swirling in clouds from the west as he entered miles of empty prairie north of Coffeyville. And good fortune befell him at the first low spot, where a ravine contained a stretch of sand and the prints made by two horses moving at a gallop.

"Maybe he'll push their horses too hard," he said into the wind hopefully. "That way I could catch sight of them before it gets dark."

He listened to the rhythmic click of iron shoes striking flint rock, and scanned an empty horizon. His muscles ached from fatigue after spending a night awake leaning against a tree, fearing sleep, which might have given Jake Willow the opportunity to slip up on him at night.

Here and there, along the skyline, he saw scattered groves of trees standing alone, seemingly out of place in a barren land where rolling flint hills could be seen for miles when he crossed high ground. While this country could be brutal, it was also a blessing for a man following hoofprints. There was no place to hide signs left by the passage of horses.

Late in the afternoon, as he rode across the tops of several hills, he thought he spotted two tiny specks in the distance to the north, although he couldn't be certain of what he saw because of the dust.

"Maybe I'm gonna get lucky before the sun goes down," he said, asking his trail-weary bay for a gallop, drumming his heels into its sides.

10

The Neosho River was low, moving sluggishly, when he rode to a grove of cottonwoods along its southern bank late in the day, after watching the river from a hilltop for several minutes with the possibility of an ambush foremost on his mind. The river lay on a featureless plain, the only landmark of any distinction for miles, precious water during a dry fall for anyone crossing eastern Kansas on a horse. When the flight of birds from treetop to treetop convinced Slocum no danger was present, he'd urged the stud downslope, staying wide of a two-rut wagon trace leading to the river. Jake Willow and the girl left their tracks in plain sight now. Apparently Willow was no longer concerned about pursuit, taking no particular pains to hide their horses' hoofprints.

The stud dropped its muzzle to the surface of the river while Slocum continued to scan the riverbanks for any sign of trouble. Late in the day the river bottom was quiet, only the scattered chirping of blue jays and sparrows interrupting an absolute silence. A flaming sunset left its red reflection on the still water, and had it not been for a manhunt pressing him onward, Slocum might have camped here for the night. It was a pretty spot, cottonwoods and drooping willows casting lengthening shadows beside the river. Deer tracks and the footprints of all manner of wildlife lay in the mud along the water's edge. And just to the north, the hoofprints of two horses continued up the dim wagon road to Uniontown, tracks Slocum would be following as soon as his bay took on a bellyful of water.

Cattails and bulrushes lined the banks. In slanting sunlight he could see perch darting among rocks in the shallows. Downstream he saw a pair of mallards swimming peacefully away from him, their bright feathers glinting in shafts of gold beaming from the horizon as they rounded a bend in the river half a mile to the east, keeping enough distance between themselves and the horseman to feel safe.

While the stud continued to drink, he pulled his bottle of whiskey from his saddlebags and took a healthy swallow, savoring the taste, wishing for more. His muscles ached from so many days in a saddle—not that he was unaccustomed to such things, for he spent as much time on the back of a horse as he did most any other place.

He thought about Pearl, remembering her soft cries in the night, her youthful body. And how easily she'd tricked him into believing in her innocence.

"She damn sure had me convinced," he mumbled after a second mouthful of whiskey. It was obvious she was no beginner when it came to robbing men. Slocum was a light sleeper. Somehow Pearl had managed to empty his pockets, find the antique dagger, and slip out of his room completely unnoticed. "What the hell. I've been played for a fool before," he said bitterly, sleeving a tiny drop of whiskey from his lips. "She'll pay for it, soon as I find her and that bastard breed. They were in on this together all along. They had me figured for a sucker, a city boy who would be easy pickings."

A gust of wind lifted dust from hills north of the river. He watched the dust idly, not paying any particular attention, when his bay suddenly lifted its head from the river, looking west with its ears pricked forward.

Slocum had turned in the saddle to see what drew the horse's interest when a ball of speeding lead sizzled past the crown of his hat.

Then the crack of a rifle sounded, far off, coming from upriver, as Slocum was diving for the ground. His stud wheeled, frightened by the sound, lunging eastward toward a cottowood thicket just before Slocum landed hard on his chest and elbows in a patch of mud and short grass at the river's edge.

"Son of a bitch!" he snapped, clawing his pistol free, even though he knew the shot had come from well beyond pistol range.

He scrambled to a crouch and raced for the trees just as a bullet kicked up a puff of dirt and sand near his feet, a second explosion echoing from a spot upstream.

Gasping for wind, startled by the suddenness of the attack, he peered around the cottonwood to look for the bushwhacker. He was sure of his identity. Jake Willow had somehow managed to lie in wait without detection, waiting long enough for wild birds coming to the river to drink to grow accustomed to his presence.

"The son of a bitch is plenty smart," Slocum whispered. "I sure as hell am glad he ain't all that good with a rifle."

Backing away from the tree carefully, Slocum dodged back and forth through the thicket until he reached his horse, settling it a moment by rubbing its neck.

"Easy, boy," he said quietly. "Those bullets weren't meant for you."

He tied the stud to a low limb and pulled his Winchester

from the saddle boot, gritting his teeth when surprise turned into rage. "Now things are even, Cut Face," he snarled with a glance upriver. "Let's see how goddamn steady your nerves are when I start sending a little lead in your direction."

He crept forward on the balls of his feet, rifle to his shoulder.

Stealth was a skill he'd learned from an old Apache years ago in Arizona—moving without seeming to move, becoming a part of your surroundings, using every tree, every shadow, every rock to hide the outline of a human form, what an enemy expected to see. Naiche was a master of illusion, having learned the art from none other than Gokaleh, the great warrior white men called Geronimo. Naiche had taught Slocum as much about Apache stealth as any white man could ever know, explaining that a white man was not attuned to the subtle rhythms of Earth Mother, the slight vibrations that were given off by every living thing, including plants and trees as well as animals. And men. Apaches, he'd said, were born into a unique harmony with Earth Mother because they were the chosen people put here by the Great Spirit, and only an Apache could truly feel those vibrations. But because of Naiche's friendship with Slocum, he'd demonstrated as much as he could of the ways Apaches stalked an enemy, techniques Slocum used now as he began advancing toward a giant willow tree on the north bank of the Neosho, leaving his hat hanging on his saddlehorn, for it would be part of an outline, a silhouette made by a human form, that Jake Willow expected to see.

Light was one of the most important factors in successfully slipping up on another, the avoidance of crossing light at almost any cost, even a dim light made by a setting sun that was blocked out by trees and brush. Shadows played tricks on a man's eyes. Staying to the shadows, no matter how far in the wrong direction they might take him, was Slocum's plan for stalking his attacker now. Time was unimportant. Willow was part Indian, and he would know many of these things himself. It was to be a contest of wits and stealth, a contest wherein one man would live and the other would die.

Slocum stepped behind a tree, remaining in its shadow for several seconds, cocking an ear, listening when nothing moved beside the river.

"He's waiting for me," Slocum said under his breath. "He thinks I'll show myself sooner or later."

Wind rustled through cattails and reeds along the riverbanks, creating a wave of motion, a distraction. Slocum's eyes narrowed, focusing on the willow tree.

When no sign of movement near the tree occurred, he went quietly to the next cottonwood, keeping the rifle to his breast to prevent its metal surfaces from reflecting sunlight.

Again, there was no movement and no sound, only the soft whisper of wind through branches and reeds, the distant call of a blue jay downriver. Hunkering down, he risked crossing an open space, remembering another duel of wits like this, down on the Rio Grande in Texas, battling a demonic Mexican revolutionary general by the name of Victoriano Valdez. . . .

The Mexican village of Nava had been a stronghold for bloody revolutionaries for years, a mountain fortress guarded by loyal men who willingly died for a cause. Approaching it in one of the highest regions of the Sierra Madres required stealth, and even more, the bravado to ride brazenly through country patrolled by *federales*. But it was not blind luck that showed him where to look for a girl held hostage by General Valdez. It was a pair of beautiful Mexican maidens, Anna and Annabella, sisters almost identically beautiful, bathing in a pool below a waterfall on the road to Saltillo.

He approached them carefully, finding them bathing naked in an isolated stream in the Sierra Madres. They covered themselves as soon as they saw him watching them from trees near the pool. But when he smiled and spoke to them in halting Spanish, both girls giggled and splashed water on him. He pulled off his boots and clothing, trying to explain that he only wanted a bath himself and that he meant them no harm. But it was soon apparent they wanted something else from him, and both wanted it at the same time.

Annabella had melon-sized breasts, a pretty oval face, with teeth so white they sparkled in the sun. Anna was slightly smaller, but with perfectly rounded hips and a waist so tiny he could encircle it with both hands, fingers touching. Only Anna spoke English, a limited number of words, yet she soon made it clear that she and her sister wanted Slocum. Annabella seemed fascinated by the size of his cock.

Anna translated for her sister. "She says she has never seen a *berga* so large."

Slocum didn't need much Spanish to know what she meant as they both came out of the pool staring at his cock.

"You swim with us?" Anna asked.

"Of course. I'd planned on it."

Annabella reached for the head of his prick with tentative fingers. *"Muy grande!"* she exclaimed.

He laughed as his prick began to swell, but it was Anna who did her best to enlarge it. She knelt down in the mud at the edge of the pool and placed the head of his cock in her mouth.

Annabella offered him one of her breasts, fondling the hard nipple herself until he took it between his teeth.

"Qúe bueno!" she cried, trembling with desire, taking him by the hand to lead him into the water up to his knees.

And for the next hour they played in the pool, until Anna led him to a grassy spot below a tree. There, he made love to both girls until he was utterly, totally spent.

But it was as they sat naked side by side on the grass that he found out what he wanted to know about the dreaded Mexican General Victoriano Valdez. Valdez made his headquarters in a little mountain village named Nava, a day's ride south of the city of Saltillo.

Anna warned that there was only one road leading up a string of mountains to the village, and that he would be watched every step of the way by armed soldiers loyal to Valdez.

Slocum couldn't tell them that a very young American girl, the daughter of a wealthy Texas rancher, was being held for ransom there by Valdez, or that he was being paid to bring her back to Texas at any cost.

Instead, he pretended to be looking for a position as a paid mercenary soldier himself, wondering if Valdez would hire an American gunman to help fight for his revolutionary cause. And it became apparent Anna and Annabella believed him, for they gave him instructions for reaching Nava, even though later he would be forced to pass himself off as someone else in order to rescue the girl.

Now he lay on his belly, crawling forward, moving through stands of grass and bushes, closing in on Jake Willow's hiding place. No more shots had been fired, and Slocum understood. Willow had missed with his first two bullets, and now he feared giving his exact position away.

Using his elbows, Slocum slithered between tree trunks and brush as soundlessly as a rattler. Very soon, Cut Face would have the chance to show John Slocum if he could live up to his reputation as a dangerous killer.

11

His senses warned him, but not in a way he expected. As he stood rock-still behind a cottonwood examining the far side of the river where the shots were fired, he felt nothing, no presence close by, no trace of the usual prickling sensation down the back of his neck. Something was wrong, something he couldn't identify, and the longer he looked at the river, the barren hills beyond it touching a purpling sky, surrounded by silence, the more the feeling grew stronger. Something was amiss, tugging at the edges of his consciousness, yet he couldn't put a finger on what it was.

Slocum turned his gaze slowly back downriver, pausing for a closer look at shadowy places, thick bulrushes, willow trees with oddly twisted trunks, anything that seemed out of place. And he still found no reason for a vague sense that things weren't right. He was a hundred yards from the tree where both shots came from, a hundred yards of shallow river and sloping banks. He'd learned to trust his senses over the years, knowing when he was very close to danger as though by instinct. So why was that feeling not with him now?

To the east, he examined the spot where he'd ridden his

horse down to drink. And at that very moment he understood how badly he'd been fooled again. The distance was
too great for any marksman to be sure of a shot. The gunfire
was meant to draw him away from his means of survival
crossing an empty plain . . . his horse.

"Son of a bitch!" he hissed, ignoring all caution now as
he began to run for the tree where his bay was tied. Either
the girl or Jake had fired at him, perhaps only hoping to get
lucky with bullets that would lure him toward the shooter
out of anger, while the other partner in this disguised ambush waited patiently for him to leave his stud.

Slocum's moccasined feet beat out a steady rhythm, racing over dry grass between cottonwoods. He made no attempt to hide, for in his heart he was sure he was too late.
Gripping the stock of his rifle fiercely, silently cursing his
carelessness, he ran as hard as he could through dusky shadows with his heart hammering inside his chest. Until he
heard another thudding noise, the drum of hoofbeats galloping off to the east.

Swinging toward higher ground that would give him a
view of land on both sides of the river, he saw what he
expected to see as night fell over the hills. Galloping east
along the southern bank of the Neosho, a slender girl riding
a sorrel was leading his bay stallion away at a headlong run,
dust flying from the horses' heels.

Slocum stumbled to a halt, blind rage welling inside him,
his lungs starving for air after a desperate run that came too
late to save his horse. And his gear, the food and water he
carried, his bedroll, shotgun, and extra ammunition.

For a moment he stood with his feet planted, sides heav-
ing, having never felt so foolish in his life. He watched Pearl
lead his horse out of sight over a hilltop, no doubt to meet
up with Jake Willow at a predetermined spot somewhere

further downriver. Not only did they have his money, just shy of a thousand dollars, and a priceless Mongol dagger inlaid with gold, but now they had his valuable Remount Thoroughbred stallion, easily a five-hundred-dollar animal to a racehorse breeder.

Finally, when the hopelessness of his situation began to sink in, he pushed all thoughts of vengeance aside for a moment to consider his chances of survival.

"I can walk the rest of the way to Uniontown," he told himself, looking north at twilight-blackened hills. But he was penniless, flat broke, with the five-dollar gold piece hidden in the lining of a stovepipe boot in his war bag tied to the saddle. He could hunt wild game along the river tonight, yet he was without matches to start a fire, and the old-time Indian method of striking flint chips in tinder was a slow process, sometimes requiring as much luck as skill unless the wind was just right, just still enough to allow a tiny flame to spring to life.

He had no real idea just how far it was to Uniontown, only a guess, perhaps fifty miles. Fort Scott was roughly fifteen miles further east, but there he could send a telegram to a friend up in Denver who could ask army brass for the loan of a horse and saddle to keep after Jake and the girl, and perhaps enough food to see Slocum through.

He took stock of his armament. A Winchester rifle with seven cartridges, six in the loading tube and one in the firing chamber. His Colt .44 held six shells, and he carried thirty in cartridge loops around his gunbelt; however, the pistol wasn't much of a hunting weapon, and if he hoped to dine on a wild turkey or a deer's hindquarter, he'd have to acquire his meal with the rifle.

He stared north again. "I can't believe I was so goddamn dumb," he muttered, lowering his head in disgust and embarrassment even though no one else was there to see his plight. He was afoot, flat broke, made to look like the fool he was for allowing himself to be tricked so easily. Again, by the same two people, a backshooting halfbreed and a gangly blond girl who knew how to use her charms to cause him to let his guard down.

Slocum looked down at his crotch once more. "You did this to me," he growled, addressing his cock. "You got stiff for the little lady, and now look where it got me."

He shook his head and half stumbled down to the river to wash his face in cool water, hoping it might also cool down his anger.

When he came to the river he knelt on a flat rock to cup water in his hands, briefly peering down at his reflection in light from the first stars of night overhead.

"You gotta be the dumbest son of a bitch on earth, Johnny boy," he said to his wavering image on the surface as currents swirled slowly past the rock. "If you had a lick of sense you'd have known what they were up to. Even Bill Cody couldn't have made that shot from so far away."

Slocum bathed his face and neck with his rifle lying beside him. The water provided no relief or distraction from the dark mood he was in. He took a few mouthfuls of water and rocked back on his haunches, pondering this latest dose of misfortune despite a desperate wish not to dwell on it, staring up at the sky.

He'd known hard times before, more than he cared to recall, and somehow he'd always found a remedy. Jake Willow and the girl were now most likely convinced their pursuit had been ended by leaving Slocum afoot.

His eyes fell to the northern horizon. "They don't know much about Calhoun County folks," he whispered savagely, while his hands balled unconsciously into fists. A different breed of men and women came from the Appalachian Mountains in Georgia, and the sons of William and Opal Slocum were known for their toughness, beginning in early childhood. Robert, older than John by two years, established a family reputation for bare-knuckling by the time he was eight, and as soon as John began to grow they quickly became a pair to be reckoned with at Saturday night barn dances, or after school. By the age of thirteen, John could look back at the last fistfight he would ever lose when pitted fairly against just one man without a hidden weapon or a club. That same toughness made the Slocum brothers virtually invincible in Calhoun County. It took a war to bring Lieutenant Robert Slocum down, a musket ball at Gettysburg, which was a fate John narrowly avoided over four bloody years of conflict. And giving up simply wasn't Slocum's style, no matter how impossible any situation seemed. Like the fix he found himself in now, alone on an empty Kansas prairie without a horse or food, miles from anywhere without a cent in his pockets, after everything he had in his possession was stolen by a pair of clever thieves.

He stood up slowly, cradling his Winchester. "It ain't over till it's over," he said quietly, "and this is a hell of a long way from being finished between us."

He found the spot where three horses crossed the river by the light of the moon, almost two miles downstream from where he had been ambushed. The tracks led north.

With water making a soft squishing sound in his moccasins after wading the river, he set out at a brisk walk along the tracks, judging the hour to be getting close to midnight.

He'd made a lucky shot, dropping a roosting prairie hen, an hour after dark, and it had taken considerable time to get a small fire going, build a spit of green sticks, and roast his fowl. Now, with his belly full, feeling rested, he followed the hoofprints in a wide arc until they came back to the wagon road a little more than five miles north of the Neosho.

At times he trotted as long as he could, until fatigue forced him to walk another mile or so, balancing the Winchester in one hand. He did his best to keep his anger in check, but there were moments when thoughts of revenge overwhelmed him. Walking across hilltops, then through shallow swales, he forced his weary legs to keep moving as hours passed.

He noted one change in his favor several hours later. The tracks were closer together, prints made by horses ridden at a walk. Jake was confident now he had eliminated any chance of being followed closely.

"Maybe it's that goddamn breed's turn to get careless," he said hopefully, breaking into a trot, pushing himself to the very limits of his endurance.

False dawn brightened skies to the east. On a faraway hilltop Slocum could make out the dim shape of an abandoned wagon listing on a broken axle, its bowlike skeletal hoops appearing as the ribs of some giant beast rising above the wagon bed. This was brutally rough country for travelers, its flint rock hard on iron wagon-wheel rims and any animal's hooves. Slocum's moccasins had thick soles of cured rawhide, although he had to be careful of large stones with sharp edges in the dark.

His limbs felt like lead weights, and now the rifle seemed as though it weighed a hundred pounds, even when he carried it on his shoulder from time to time. Walking and trotting all night reminded him of forced marches with Jackson for the Confederacy, for conditions were much the same: poor rations, a heavy musket, and seemingly endless miles to travel before Jackson led them into another engagement, almost always one-sided, a Rebel army outnumbered by as much as five or six to one charging toward a better-equipped Union force with full bellies and plenty of ammunition, including cannons loaded with canisters of grapeshot that cut men to shreds at almost any range.

"I reckon things could be worse," Slocum told himself as he climbed a hill toward the abandoned wagon. "At least for now, nobody's shooting at me."

He found a pleasant surprise beside the wagon, although his nose told him what to expect long before he got there. Blackened remains of a campfire still had glowing embers at the center of its firepit.

"They got hungry," he said, stirring the coals with a stick. "Hadn't been but a few hours . . . three or four."

He scanned a lightening horizon to the north. Not many hours away, Jake Willow and Pearl were taking their time moving toward Uniontown. He glanced down at an empty tin of peaches and felt hunger gnaw his belly, thinking of their sweet taste until he started forward again at a trot.

"Won't nothing be as sweet as having a day of reckoning with the two of you," he whispered, hoping Willow's cruelty did not extend to animals. "If that bay stud is harmed in any way, you've got my word I'm gonna make you suffer, asshole."

He ran down a steeper grade to the bottom of a ravine where the road crossed to the next bald knob. Slocum had no strength left to run uphill; thus, he settled for a slower gait until he reached the top.

The first golden rays of sunshine beamed over hills to the east, illuminating the prairie by slow degrees as he trotted onward, resting the Winchester across his shoulder. He could only guess how far he'd come during the night. Sometime late in the morning, perhaps close to noon, he'd make Uniontown. If his weary legs could keep up the pace.

12

Uniontown could hardly be called a town. It was a settlement of sod houses and a single store built from clapboard planking weathered by wind and sun. A road running eastward from Fort Scott to the railhead at Wichita gave the settlement a reason to exist, for it had water, a few wood-bladed windmills rising from the flats providing a bounty for thirsty travelers and their animals. As Slocum walked on numbed legs over a swell in the prairie, he saw Uniontown and summoned the last reserves of strength he had as he stumbled down a gentle slope toward the flats and water. His mouth was so dry, his lips were cracked after hours walking under a merciless sun, bent into a northwesterly wind that never seemed to end and that blasted gritty particles into his eyes. His feet had begun to throb with deep stone bruises, and he wondered if he would be able to walk to Fort Scott and a telegraph, where he could wire Colonel Jim Thompson at Fort Lupton, just north of Denver, requesting assistance. He'd known Colonel Thompson for years, and Jim trusted Slocum from his stints as a scout for army patrols during the worst of the Indian wars there.

Slocum could see lumbering freight wagons moving westward and one or two heading east. Perhaps he could beg a ride on one of the wagons to Fort Scott ferrying supplies to the army. At the moment he didn't think he could manage another twelve to fifteen miles on sore feet. His fate lay in the hands of an understanding teamster traveling east.

The small size of Uniontown left Slocum feeling sure that Jake and Pearl had moved on toward Kansas City, after watering their horses. Even with a poke full of money, a place like Uniontown offered nothing in the way of pleasant diversions for either the halfbreed or the girl. Thus he made his slow-footed approach without any particular caution, after making sure his big bay stud or the horses Willow and Pearl were riding weren't in any of the corrals near the sod dwellings or behind the store. He was shading his eyes from the sun with his hand after leaving his hat on his saddlehorn before the bay was stolen. He remembered seeing Pearl wearing a hat as she rode off leading the stud, and he concluded it must have been his.

"They moved on," he mumbled, running his tongue over split lips, rubbing dust from his eyes. "I'll lose another five or six hours heading over to Fort Scott, but there ain't no choice under present circumstances. I damn sure can't walk to Kansas City on these legs."

Following the ruts, he made his way down to the settlement with one eye on a water trough beneath a windmill. A short length of pipe dribbled water into a big circular tank fashioned from mortar and stone. Before he attended to the business of getting to Fort Scott, he meant to drink his fill and find a patch of shade where he could rest a moment.

Water had seldom tasted so good as when he drank from the pipe, listening to the rattle of a sucker rod drawing the water from the well. An old man with silver whiskers, dressed in a pair of mended overalls, watched him drink from the shade of a thatched porch in back of a sod house.

"You lose yer hoss to a rattler or a broke leg?" the old man asked.

Slocum looked up. "A two-legged rattler. My horse was stolen back at the Neosho River last night."

"That's damn near fifty mile, son. You done a hell of a lot of walkin'."

"You get no argument outa me, mister. Seemed more like a hundred, those last few miles." He sleeved water off his mouth and turned around. "Did you happen to see a man and a woman ride through here today? They'd be leading an extra horse. One's a black, another's a sorrel, and a big bay stud."

"Sure did. Come in early this mornin'. Stopped at Willard's Store over yonder an' bought a few things. Not yer ordinary things neither. The woman bought a sack plumb full of candy sticks. The dark-skinned feller with the scar bought two bottles of whiskey an' some tins of tomaters an' peaches. Sure did look like them hosses had been rode hard. They the ones who stole yer hoss?"

"That's them, all right. Which way did they ride when they left?"

"North. Right up that road yonder to Mound City. Didn't act like they was in no particular hurry, like folks who done a touch of hoss stealin' oughta act."

Slocum looked at the road the old man indicated. It was more of the same, a single pair of ruts that saw little use winding up from the flats around Uniontown. "How far is it to Fort Scott?" he asked.

"Less'n a dozen miles. Ain't much distance fer a man on a hoss, but it's a hell of a stretch fer a gent without one. You look kinda spent, stranger. If'n I was you I wouldn't strike out fer Fort Scott in them little bitty Injun shoes. I seen you when you came walkin' in. You're damn near as sore-footed as a road-foundered mule.''

''I'd planned to hitch a ride on one of those freight wagons if I could,'' he explained, feeling somewhat better after a drink and a moment's rest. ''I can wire a friend of mine at an army post up in Colorado, to arrange for borrowing an army mount so I can stay after the pair who stole my stud.''

The old man pushed himself up off a bench resting against the wall of his house, peering around a corner. ''Yonder's an empty wagon owned by Cleve Brooks. The driver'll be glad to take you to the fort soon as he's watered his mules an' bought hisself a jug of red-eye. The mule skinner's name is Bullwhip Jones, an' if you was to ask, he'd take you, I reckon.''

''I'm much obliged,'' Slocum answered, eyeing a big Studebaker and two spans of mules parked in front of the store. The wagon's canvas cover was laden with dust, as were the mules. It appeared the wagon had come a considerable distance.

As he was walking away from the shadow beneath the windmill, he heard the man say, ''Maybe you oughta give it some thought, stranger, chasin' after that feller who stole yer hoss. It don't appear you've done too good in yer dealin's with him so far. I'd let the law handle it, if'n I was you.''

Slocum ingored the remark and aimed for the Studebaker, catching sight of a thick-shouldered man in baggy pants applying grease to wagon hubs on the far side. Slocum ambled up to the wagon and stood there a moment until he caught the teamster's eye.

''Name's John Slocum,'' he began, resting his rifle against one wheel. ''An old man behind that windmill said

I might ask you for a ride to Fort Scott. He told me you were called Bullwhip Jones.''

Jones nodded, his sun-darkened face expressionless as he gave Slocum a closer look. ''Fixin' to leave jus' now,'' he said as he dropped a clothbound stick in his grease bucket. ''You kin ride with me. Takes a couple of hours to git there.''

''I'd be real grateful. I lost my horse to a thief down on the Neosho last night and I need to make arrangements for another mount at the fort.''

Jones whistled through tobacco-stained teeth. ''You done a bunch of walkin', mister. Climb up in that seat yonder an' we'll git started. I got a soft spot fer a feller fallen on hard times seein' as I've had a few myself. There's a jug o' panther piss under the seat in a burlap bag. You look like you could use a drink or two.''

It didn't matter right then how bad the whiskey was that Jones was offering him. If it was truly distilled panther piss, he meant to drink it anyway. ''I'm in your debt,'' he said, taking his rifle and climbing slowly, painfully up a front wagon wheel with the soles of his feet aching fiercely.

Gazing east, he watched wagon traffic on the road to Fort Scott send up clouds of chalky dust. This would be another delay, giving Jake Willow and Pearl more time to elude him. It had begun to seem that every possible twist of black fate had befallen him since he'd ridden into Fort Smith to deliver a present on behalf of a friend. He'd think better of offering his services in similar fashion the next time.

Colonel Wilson Rogers sported red sideburns and a trimmed beard. He shook hands with Slocum in his office at Fort Scott with a doubtful look on his face.

''Take a chair, Mr. Slocum, and tell me again what you

want from me and how it is you know Colonel James Thompson.''

Slocum eased his weight into a wood chair. ''Jim and I are old friends. I did some scouting for his command a few years back. I was robbed of my money and a valuable antique dagger in Fort Smith. When I set out to follow the pair who did it, they stole my horse.''

''Sounds to me like this is a matter for the law. You should have informed territorial marshals.''

''I talked to Marshal Heck Thomas in Fort Smith. They were shorthanded, so I took matters into my own hands.''

Rogers frowned. ''It doesn't sound like you've done too well at it. Parts of these western territories are full of desperate men who'll do most anything, with no respect for the law. I can notify the marshal's office up in Kansas City.''

''That'll be fine, Colonel, but I'd ask that you wire Colonel Thompson about me, and I assure you he'll tell you I can be trusted with a horse and saddle. I can have money sent by Wells Fargo to pay for the animal, but the longer I wait the farther away those two will get. I need to stay on their tracks while they're fresh.''

Rogers hesitated, glancing out a window at the parade ground inside the stockade. ''It's a civilian matter, but I suppose I can send out a patrol to look for these two men.''

''One's a woman, a girl,'' Slocum explained. ''About all I know about her is her first name. She calls herself Pearl.''

''A woman?'' The colonel sounded surprised.

''She set me up for the robbery. Jake Willow was in on it with her. They call him Cut Face because of a scar—''

Rogers waved a hand. ''We know about him. He's a half-breed Cherokee. He's on a list of names the territorial marshals sent us. He's suspected of several murders, I think. Once again, it is a civilian matter under territorial jurisdiction, and unless I get orders to arrest him for a specific federal charge, my hands are tied.''

''All I'm asking for is a good horse and a saddle.'' Slocum grinned. ''Maybe a bite to eat. All my foodstuffs were on my horse when they stole him. If you'll only send a wire to Colonel Thompson, he'll vouch for me . . . for my honesty. I'll return the horse and saddle as soon as I get mine back.''

''We've got regulations. I'd be sticking my neck out. If you'll contact the proper authorities, they can look for Willow and his female accomplice legally. I can't just loan a horse to every civilian who walks through these gates. There are regulations, you know.''

Slocum was so near complete exhaustion he almost lost his temper. ''If you'd only wire Jim Thompson, he'll find a way to get the army's permission.''

Rogers closed his eyes briefly. ''I'll wire Fort Lupton, but that's all I'll promise you. In the meantime, you can go over to the mess and get something to eat. Sergeant Phillips will take you there.''

It was the best he could hope for, facing a soldier who went by the book like Rogers. ''I'd appreciate it, the telegram and the food.''

He got up slowly, wincing when his feet hurt him, and gave the colonel his hand. ''Thanks. I'll ask the sergeant to show me to the mess and then I'll wait outside some place. Maybe grab a few minutes of sleep.''

Rogers shook his head. ''Sorry, Mr. Slocum, but this is all I can do.''

''I understand,'' Slocum said without feeling, turning for the door leading to an outer officer where Sergeant Phillips sat at his desk.

∙ ∙ ∙

He was sound asleep in a shaded corner of a porch across the front of fort headquarters when a voice woke him up.

"That you, Slocum?"

He raised his head sleepily, blinking, trying to see who it was that spoke to him. A cavalry patrol trotted across the fort's compound, riding in through the fort gates.

He saw a blurred face, a tangled gray beard and hair hanging over a small man's shoulders. He didn't recognize the face or the voice right then. He was still only half awake, his brain clogged by sleep fog. "I'm John Slocum. Who are you?"

A toothless grin stretched the man's webbed face. "I'll be damn. You don't remember me?"

Slocum sat up, rubbing his eyes. "Can't say as I..." Then he chuckled, shaking his head. "Can that be you, Dale Moss? I heard you were dead."

The old man's grin widened. "Hell, I figured I was dead myself, till I found out I was only in Kansas. This has got to be the ugliest place God ever made. Hell can't be no hotter or no drier." He held out a gnarled hand.

Slocum shook with Moss and came slowly to his feet. He and Dale Moss had once scouted together for the army out of Fort Grant in Arizona. "Well, you damn sure ain't dead," Slocum said, grinning his own wide grin. "You're a sight for sore eyes. What the hell are you doing at Fort Scott, pardner?"

"Scoutin' fer this bunch of greenhorns. They ain't got a man who can find his ass with both hands in this whole outfit. Now I'm gonna ask the same damn question . . . what the hell are you doin' here?"

"It's a long story. I was robbed of a thousand dollars and my horse got stolen."

Hearing this, Moss laughed out loud. "You? John Slocum

got robbed an' put afoot?'' His expression turned serious at once. ''I feel sorry for the pore son of a bitch who done it. You're gonna kill him, ain't you?''

''I've got to find him first. I need a horse and a saddle real bad, a good horse that can cover some ground.''

Moss nodded, aiming a thumb over his shoulder. ''I've got three in my string. You can take your pick. Only, I've got this big buttermilk roan that can outrun the wind, an' he can do it all day long. He's cold-backed in the mornin' an' he'll try to buck you off. He'll kick you harder'n any mule if you walk behind him, but I never owned a better trail horse. But then I reckon you know horses well as me. Sometimes the meaner they are, the better they are. Take the roan, an' you're welcome to my spare saddle. It's a little dog-eared, like me, but you can set it an' it won't put no blisters on your ass.''

''Damn!'' Slocum whispered, eyeing Moss as though he'd found an oasis in the desert. ''Maybe my luck's about to change. I'll find a way to make it up to you.''

Moss stepped back from the porch, scratching his beard. ''You won't owe me nothin','' he said, ''but I know damn well you musta been drunk when your troubles happened. Any idea who done it to you?''

''They call him Cut Face Jake Willow. He's got a girl with him.''

Moss nodded. ''I've heard the name. One thing I already do know 'bout him. His name's about to change. Pretty quick they'll be callin' him Dead Cut Face Jake Willow, soon as you catch up to him. Follow me over to the stable an' I'll show you the roan. Knowin' you like I do, I got it figured you've got this itch to git started afore the trail turns cold.''

13

"He ain't none too pretty to look at, I'd agree," Moss said as Slocum cinched an old high-horned mountain saddle to the back of a rawboned milky roan gelding as quickly as he could, taking note of the horse's oversized head and Roman nose, a rounded eye warning of trouble coming when he climbed on the horse's back.

"He's just what I need," Slocum replied. Despite the animal's ugly appearance, it had long pasterns, a sloping croup, and just enough muscle in the gaskins and stifle joints to be a runner with considerable speed. "Some of the best wives are ugly women. What I'm needing him for ain't beauty."

Moss chuckled. "Like I said, he'll buck when you step up on his hurricane deck, but it's only a few jumps, to see if he can unseat you. Soon as he finds out you aim to stay there, he'll give up an' act like a horse is supposed to. Remember what I said 'bout his hind legs. Sumbitch can kick harder'n any mule, an' I'd nearly swear he enjoys it if he gits a lick in on one of yer kneecaps. Folks claim a horse can't grin, but I swear this sumbitch does after he kicks you." Without teeth, Moss's words sounded mushy at times.

The roan had a noticeable hump in its back when Slocum got the cinch tight. "We'll get along. I'll bring him back to you as soon as I catch up to Willow and get my belongings back." He stuck his Winchester in the saddle's empty rifle boot.

"Which way's he headed, Slocum?"

"North. I figure they're bound for Kansas City." He led the roan out of the stable with Moss walking beside him. "If I have any luck, maybe I can catch 'em before they get there."

"There's two of 'em? Hell, why didn't you say so. I'll saddle a fresh horse an' ride with you. It'll be like the old days down in Arizona. I scout fer this damn army whenever it suits me, an' it just stopped suitin' me when you said there was two of them horse thieves."

"No need," Slocum said, halting the roan at the edge of the parade ground. "One's a girl. I can handle it myself."

Moss scowled, reading Slocum's face. "Sometimes there just ain't nothin' no more dangerous than a damn female. I'll ride along anyways, if you got no objections. You an' me have got a lot of catchin' up to do."

Dale Moss was an expert tracker, Slocum remembered, and a deadly shot at great distances with a Sharps buffalo gun he used to carry. "You're welcome to ride with me, but there's no need on my account," he said, cheeking the roan's bridle as he stuck his left foot in a stirrup, preparing for the first powerful jump when the horse started bucking.

"Won't be but a minute," Moss said, hurrying back into the stable on badly bowed legs. "I'll fetch my Palouse an' be right with you, soon as I git him saddled an' tie on my camp fixin's."

Slocum smiled inwardly. Moss knew horses as well as reading tracks.

Slocum swung up on the roan's back, and just got his right foot in the stirrup when the gelding lunged, pitching forward as it lowered its head despite the pull Slocum exerted on its reins. As the horse jumped, it let out a mighty bawling sound. Then it landed hard on its forefeet and bucked skyward again.

Slocum let the roan make one more jump before he jerked the right rein, swinging the gelding around in a tight circle. The moment it felt the bite of an iron bit in its mouth, it simply stopped bucking and lowered its head, snorting once.

He grinned. "You aren't as bad as all that," he said as he gave the horse a pat on the neck. "Maybe your owner is a little long in the tooth to be riding a pitching horse."

While he waited for Moss to get saddled, he thought back to their days at Fort Grant, scouting for Cochise and his band of Apaches. This was before Geronimo became a war leader, a time when Arizona Territory was unsettled, empty, bristling with Apache warriors on the prowl. It was there where Slocum had made a friend of Naiche, learning many things about Indians he hadn't known before, including a respect for their fierce loyalty to each other and their fighting prowess.

Moss came out of the barn leading a blanket-hipped Palouse gelding, a black roan in front with a snow-white rump. He gave Slocum a nod. "I see you got the hump out of his back. Soon as I stop at headquarters to tell Colonel Rogers where I'm off to, we'll be on our way. Hell, this is gonna be like old times, Slocum, just you an' me in lonesome country followin' horse sign plumb to eternity, if that's where it takes us."

Slocum gazed north. "I figure eternity is gonna be Kansas City, if we don't catch up beforehand. One thing's for damn sure, and that's I'm not stopping until I find them."

Moss climbed stiffly into his saddle. Slocum guessed his age at close to sixty by now, old for any man to be in a saddle all day.

Moss collected his reins while the Palouse stood quietly. "Like I told you before, I feel sorry for the pore son of a bitch when we do, 'cause I know yer gonna kill him. He don't know it yet, but he's a dead man, sure as snuff makes spit."

Riding cross-country, they made the twenty-three miles to Mound City by late afternoon, pushing their horses hard to make up for lost time, exchanging few words in their haste. Slocum was pleased by the buttermilk roan's long, easy strides, and he noted Moss's Palouse had no shortage of stamina or speed. In a way it was good to be riding with Dale Moss again, even though the reason for it wasn't sitting well in Slocum's craw. But to make the best of things he pushed thoughts of Jake Willow and Pearl from his mind to keep his anger in check for the present.

Mound City was much like Uniontown, a few sod houses, a store built of wood planks, and three windmills, another settlement too small to have a telegraph line. They rode into town at a gallop and reined down in front of the store.

"I'll ask if they came through," Slocum said, dropping to the ground and handing Moss his reins.

"I'll water these winded broncs," Moss told him, swinging toward a windmill behind the store.

Slocum climbed a set of steps and went inside, finding an old woman smiling at him expectantly behind a glass-topped counter.

"What'll it be, mister?" she asked, taking a quick look at his gun.

"Just some information, ma'am. Did a man with a scar

on his face come through here with a woman today?''

The woman's smile left her face. ''They certainly did. He was an awful man, and he'd beaten that poor girl something terrible. She had a big bruise on her cheek and her mouth was bleedin'. They watered their horses an' he bought tobacco, I think. If we had a lawman I'd have told him about what was done to the girl. A shame . . . they rode off north, toward Paola.''

''About how long ago?'' he asked, wondering what could have prompted Willow to strike Pearl.

''Not long. Round noon, I reckon. The man acted drunk to me, smellin' of whiskey real strong. He was rude about it when he asked for makin's for smokes. Had a whole pocketful of money, only he only bought tobacco with it. The girl stood over in a corner an' didn't say nary a word, like she was scared to death to open her mouth. A shame is what it was, the way she looked when she came inside.''

''Thank you,'' Slocum said as he made for the door, his hopes higher now. Willow must have stopped somewhere for a rest, or to drink whiskey, perhaps have his way with Pearl while he was drunk enough to feel the need to slap her around.

He found Moss watering their horses at the back of the store and said, ''They were here four or five hours ago, according to the lady inside. Headed north toward a place called Paola.''

''Just across the Marias River,'' Moss replied knowingly as he looked that direction. ''Rough flint country till we git to that creek, where the land softens some. Be easier to track 'em north of the Marias. Maybe they'll stop at the river tonight. If they do, this hunt is nearly over. We'll git there afore midnight if we ride hard.''

''That's just what I aim to do,'' Slocum answered, checking the cinch on the roan before he mounted. "Ride hard and do a little squaring of accounts when we find them, if we get lucky enough tonight."

Moss had a chaw of tobacco in his cheek. He spat before he swung his Palouse away from the water trough. "I've got me a notion or two 'bout luck, Slocum. A man usually makes his own luck, one way or the other. Let's push these broncs as hard as we can while it's daylight. We'll keep from havin' any bad luck tonight if we go slow after it gits dark."

They rode out of Mound City at a lope, riding side by side toward distant flint hills, the clatter of horseshoes on rock making a noise Slocum knew would be a handicap during the quiet hours of darkness.

A sky like black velvet hanging above the twisting course of a dark tree-lined river, made visible by light from the moon and stars, greeted them as they rode at a walk to the crest of the river valley.

"Yonder she is," Moss said softly, letting his gaze wander the length of the river that they could see. "Tracks lead straight thataway, Slocum. He's prob'ly too smart to build much of a fire out in the open, bein' he's a breed. Dug a firepit, most likely, an' smothered it when he was done. Don't smell no smoke from up here."

"He's smart," Slocum agreed, giving the river a similar close inspection. "Maybe we'll smell smoke when we get closer."

"There's a chance they rode on," Moss warned, standing in his stirrups to look at something to the west. "If we split up we can cover more country."

"This isn't your fight," Slocum said. "Wait here for me and I'll ride down."

Moss wagged his head. "Bullshit. Any fight yer in is part mine when I'm sidin' you. I'll ride east an' come back this way whilst you cover the west end of the valley. If it was me, I'd have crossed over first. It ain't hardly more'n a creek, but it's water an' horses don't leave no tracks. I'll give a coyote call when I see you comin', so you'll know it's me. If you hear any shootin', come a-runnin'."

Before Slocum could offer any further objections, Moss turned his horse, heading down into the valley in an easterly direction with his modified Walker Colt .44 drawn, resting the barrel on the cantle of his saddle.

Reining west, Slocum began a slow descent toward the Marias, annoyed by the clatter of iron when the roan crossed rock, for it would be like a beacon to Jake Willow when he heard it, certain to draw his gunfire. And it was no help to be riding a light-colored horse at night. The roan's coat caught too much moonlight, drawing attention to Slocum's approach.

And now he felt it, the sensation of being close to his prey as the hairs prickled down the back of his neck. In a way he could never describe, he knew Willow was close by, perhaps just a stone's throw across the river.

He took the hammer thong off his Colt and readied it for a quick pull. "I can damn near smell you, you son of a bitch," he said in a hoarse whisper.

The dark outlines of cottowood trees lining the bank of the river stood like giant hands reaching skyward in the night. He scented the air and found nothing on the winds, no trace of smoke or the more pungent smell of burned-out ashes. He worried some about Dale Moss putting his life on the line for him, yet he knew Moss well enough to know he couldn't be talked out of throwing in even when it wasn't his fight.

"Old Moss can handle himself with the best of 'em," he said aloud, guiding the roan around a slab of flint. Moss still had keen eyes, even if his joints did work a little slower than they had in the past.

The click of the roan's shoes seemed to grow louder, although Slocum judged it was probably only his imagination making him feel this way now, when silence could prove to be the difference between living and dying.

Once, he glanced over his shoulder, after he'd ridden about a quarter mile upriver. Moss was lost in a sea of darkness, and Slocum felt some better about things.

Somewhere in the night an owl hooted. In Apache country it could have been a warning call made by an Indian, but with Jake Willow on the run in unfamiliar country, he wouldn't be imitating the owl's cry. But what the owl's voice *did* say about the land ahead of Slocum was that it was empty. An owl would not make its call if a human was close.

The further to the west he rode, the more he began to lose the sensation of danger. He hauled back on the horse's reins to look both ways, listening, flaring his nostrils to pick up any scent. For a time he sat there, waiting, harkening to his senses, feeling something was wrong.

"I'm riding the wrong direction," he said under his breath as he gave the eastern horizon a lingering stare. "I can damn near feel it in my bones."

Proof of his assumption came suddenly. A distant gunshot echoed from the east, followed by two more in rapid succession.

"Damn!" he hissed, jerking the roan around, drumming his heels into its sides.

14

The rumbling of the roan's pounding hooves would warn Jake Willow of his rapid approach and make him a target, but with the chance Dale Moss might take a bullet meant for him, Slocum rode hell-for-leather toward the gunshots without a thought for his own safety. Bending low over the horse's neck, his Colt .44 clamped in his right fist, he charged toward the sounds, asking the roan for everything it had. In the darkness he could only see shapes where moonlight brightened open land, but in the row of trees on both sides of the river shadows were deep, black as pitch, revealing nothing. There was no sign of Moss's horse or any movement Slocum could discern among the cotton-woods, and for the moment Slocum was riding blind. He couldn't see across the river, with the far side blocked by stands of trees. It occurred to him he might be galloping straight toward a well-placed chunk of lead, and with that thought in mind, he slowed the gelding some, holding it in a steady lope.

A half mile ahead, he caught a glimpse of a white-rumped pony trotting away from the river, and by far the worst part of the sight was an empty saddle cinched to Moss's Palouse.

Maybe he'd jumped for cover, Slocum thought. Moss had always been clever, hard to kill even when Cochise sent his best warriors after army scouts to slow pursuing columns of cavalry. But seeing Moss's saddle empty made something twist in Slocum's belly, and he could only hope for the best until he got there. Glancing at dark trees and shadows to his right, Slocum kept riding with his mouth set in a grim line. He was almost certain the first shot he'd heard had come from a rifle, the next pair fired by a pistol, and what those sounds told him he didn't like. Willow had fired first from ambush. The next shots had probably come from Moss's Walker.

Willow wasn't that good with a rifle when he fired at me at the Neosho, Slocum remembered. Maybe he missed Moss and the old man dismounted in a hurry to hide himself in the cottonwoods.

Slocum pulled the roan down to a trot when he neared the wandering Palouse, and instantly, his eyes and nose told him the ugly truth of what had happened. A dark stain glimmered sticky and wet over the Palouse's rump, and it smelled coppery, of blood.

He reined to a sliding stop beside the Palouse while staring at the river, and now his ears added more information to what he already knew. Off to the north he heard the clatter of iron on rock, riders moving away from the Marias at a gallop.

"You bastard," Slocum breathed, desperate for one chance to face Jake Willow out in the open. Then he turned all his attention to finding Dale Moss, leading the Palouse slowly down to the river. The bloodstain said everything. Moss, even with all his years of experience, had been shot from ambush, and by the size of the bloodstain, he was mortally wounded. Or dead.

The sounds made by the horses he rode and led blotted out the rattle of hoofbeats across the river. He rode closer to the trees, then eastward, searching for Moss among shadows near the water's edge. His sudden anger was replaced by sorrow and regret for having allowed an old friend to put himself in the gunsights of a killer gunning for *him*. With a heavy heart, knowing what he would find, he began combing the riverbank, holding his horse to a walk.

He spotted a lumpy form a hundred yards away, lying in the grass near a tall cottonwood. He drove his heels into the roan and galloped over to the spot, leaping from the saddle to kneel beside the body of Dale Moss. A dark stain covered the front of his buckskin shirt, surrounding a hole the size of Slocum's thumb.

"You're still alive," he whispered when he saw Moss's chest rise and fall slowly. Moss's eyes were closed and he appeared to be unconscious. Blood covered the grass where he lay, still leaking from the bullet hole in his chest.

Slocum lifted the old man in his arms gently, walking toward the river where mud would provide a softer place to put him down. A knot grew larger in Slocum's stomach. The bullet hole was in a bad place, on his right side near his liver. Dying gutshot was a hell of a painful way to go, he recalled from the war. Moss didn't deserve to die like this, as he surely would when internal bleeding couldn't be stopped.

Slocum found a spot beside the river with soft ground and laid Moss down. He spoke to him even though he was certain the old man couldn't hear him. "I'll go collect the horses and see if you've got anything in your camp gear . . . a bottle of whiskey to help with the pain and some cloth to bandage that wound."

He left quickly to retrieve their horses, feeling the weight of what had happened resting on his shoulders. Slocum knew his anger would become a fiery rage later on, but now, as Moss lay dying, the only emotion he had was an overwhelming sense of deep sorrow.

He returned and tied the horses in trees near the river before he went through Moss's saddlebags, discovering a half-empty pint bottle of white moonshine whiskey. An old shirt could be fashioned into a bandage, although in his heart Slocum knew it was a waste. Moss would die, and there were times when some gut wounds took days of pain to claim a victim.

When he reached Moss's side the old man's eyes were open, staring up at the night sky, lightly glazed with pain.

"Hey, pardner," Slocum said, kneeling beside him. "Can you hear me?"

"I can . . . hear," he croaked, turning his gaze to Slocum's face. "Tell me straight . . . how . . . bad . . . is it?"

He couldn't lie to a friend. "It's bad. Went in near your liver. Passed clean through."

Moss blinked and looked at the sky again. "Then I'm a dead son . . . of . . . a bitch, ain't I?"

"I'm no doctor."

"Don't try an' . . . bullshit me. A slug . . . through my gizzard is . . . the end of it."

"I tried to get you to stay on that rise, pardner. This was my fight. I haven't got the words to tell you how I feel right now. I'd trade places if we could. You gave me a horse and came with me when it wasn't none of your affair, and now you're paying the ultimate price for being my friend."

Slowly, feebly, Moss reached for Slocum's forearm. "Comes a time . . . when a man's . . . ready to die, Slocum. You git too old . . . to do what . . . you used to do. Got no teeth left. My dick . . . won't git hard no more. My bones ache . . . all the time. Got no family. Nobody who . . . gives a damn 'bout me.''

"I give a damn," Slocum said. "All this is my fault. I let you take a bullet with my name written on it. What I did was wrong, letting you ride with me, only I can't change it now. I wish to hell I could.''

"Save yer speeches," Moss gasped, tightening his grip on Slocum's arm. His eyes batted shut, yet he continued to breathe in shallow fashion, his thin chest barely rising and falling as his nostrils flared.

"Damn," Slocum whispered as Moss's fingers relaxed on his forearm. He took a drink of the whiskey himself, then added a splash into the bullet hole in Moss's side, sometimes a remedy for superficial wounds to keep them from festering so much, a waste of time on an injury like this.

Later, he sat beside his friend and stared across the flat surface of the river, blaming himself for what had happened, at the same time knowing it would do no good to place blame now. Moss was certain to die.

His thoughts were interrupted by two noises, a faint cry from across the river and one of the horses snorting when it heard the sound.

"What the hell?" Slocum jumped to his feet, drawing his Colt. It was a human voice, high-pitched, a call of distress. It came from upriver, not far away.

He was bewildered by it, thinking he and Moss were alone after Jake and Pearl had made their escape. He crept into the water with his pistol leveled, hunkered down, puzzled.

Inching across the slippery river bottom, he came out on the far side and stepped carefully between trees, his moccasins making soft, wet noises.

In a tiny opening near the river he came upon a most

unexpected sight. Someone was on a blanket, bound hand and foot, twisting and turning to free tied wrists from a length of rope.

A second later he recognized Pearl in the moonlight. She struggled to unfasten her hands tied behind her as she sat on the blanket beside a saddle.

When he was sure he wasn't walking into another trap set by Jake Willow, he walked away from a cottonwood trunk to reach the girl. She saw him coming and ended her struggles, watching him come closer.

He stood over her for a time without saying a word, his gun aimed down at her. "Seems ol' Cut Face can be hard on his women every now and then," he said evenly, holstering his pistol.

Pearl was crying, and even in the dark he could see dark bruises on her face. "He whupped me. He took all your money an' that fancy knife. I ain't got nothin' that belongs to you."

"Were you a bad girl?" Slocum asked, enjoying himself in a strange way while facing the woman who'd robbed him.

"He got drunk," Pearl whimpered, looking away. "He said I was nothin' but a piece of white trash."

"It may be the first thing he and I would agree on," Slocum told her.

She looked at him again. "Jake put me up to it, to rob you that night. Wasn't my idea. I done it 'cause he told me to, or he said he'd hurt me if I didn't do like he said."

"Not a very convincing story, Pearl. You'll have to do a hell of a lot better to convince me."

"It's the truth."

"I doubt it. Maybe he got worried you'd rob him, so he tied you up and left you here."

"That ain't so!" she exclaimed.

He almost felt like laughing, until he remembered Dale Moss. "Jake shot the wrong man a few minutes ago. An old friend of mine is dying over yonder across that river on account of Jake Willow."

"He thought it was the law," Pearl said.

"It wasn't. Only a man and his friend trying to get my money and horse and the dagger back that you stole from me. He won't get far."

"I hope you kill him," Pearl snapped angrily. "You can see what he done to me."

"It won't be because of what he did to you. Fact is, you had it coming."

"He swore he'd hurt me real bad 'less I helped him rob you that night."

"All that innocence you put on, it was all an act to make me trust you."

"I was scared. You don't know Jake. He's awful mean when he's drunk."

"What the hell were you doing with him in the first place, Pearl?"

"My man ran out on me. Said he was goin' to Texas. He took our wagon an' said he'd send for me, only he took up with this whore down there."

"I was told about it. Dan Willis was his name, if I remember right."

"That was him. He lied to me."

"And you lied to me."

"Jake made me do it. Can't you see what he done to my face after he got drunk?"

"You'll live, which is more than can be said for a good man by the name of Dale Moss lying over yonder. He's gonna die a real painful death on account of Jake."

"I hope you find Jake an' kill him dead. Ain't you gonna untie me?"

"Why should I?" Slocum asked. "I'd only be taking the chance you'd rob me again."

"I never woulda done it if Jake hadn't made me do it. How come you don't believe me?"

"Because you've lied to me before, you rotten little bitch, and nobody gets a second chance at me." Slocum looked north for a moment. "I guess he took all the horses too."

"He took a real fancy to your bay stallion. He told me right after he come runnin' back to camp he was gonna leave me here for the law to find. Like I told you, he figured you was the law. When he made me take your horse the other night he said that was the end of you, that a man on foot in that country was as good as dead, 'less somebody found you. He didn't act worried 'bout you, only that the law was after us . . . after him."

Slocum took a look over his shoulder at the river, thinking of Moss. "I'll untie your feet so you can walk back with me, but if you run I promise I'll hogtie you and leave you here. Is that understood?"

She nodded.

"I'm gonna tie you up again as soon as we're across the river," he said. "I don't trust you any farther'n I can throw you, bitch."

"I gotta take a pee," she said as he was kneeling down to unfasten a rope around her ankles.

He stared into her eyes. "You can piss in your pants for all I care, but you ain't leaving my sight. Remember what I said just now. If you try to run, it'll go hard on you."

15

Pearl had some difficulty walking on slippery rock through knee-deep water with her hands tied behind her. Moss was shivering when they finally crossed the river. As soon as Slocum saw him with the shakes, he took a blanket down from the back of the Palouse and covered the old man with it. Moss was still unconscious.

Slocum turned to Pearl. "Sit down," he ordered, pointing to a rock. In light from the moon he could see more of her face and the marks Jake had left on her. She wore a pair of men's pants and a torn blue shirt with buttons ripped open revealing parts of her inner breasts and one hardened nipple. "If you move I'll tie you to one of these damn trees. I won't warn you but once."

She was staring at Moss. "That's your friend, ain't it? The one Jake shot."

"As good a friend as I ever rode the trails with. They don't come any better than Dale Moss."

"He's gonna die, ain't he?"

Slocum looked down at Moss's face. "He's gutshot. Takes a long time for a man to die this way. Painful as hell too. When I do catch up to Jake I'm gonna make him suffer, like he did to my friend here.''

"I hope you kill him. He ain't no good. Mean to the core, an' he ain't got no loyalty to nobody. I hope I get the chance to watch him die slow. I'm gonna laugh loud as I can if I get to see it.'' She looked up at Slocum. "Trouble is, I don't see no way for you to catch him, an' if you do he'll most likely kill you, 'stead of the other way round. You ain't never seen nobody so good at killin' folks. He don't have no feelin's about it at all. I knowed all along he'd kill me any time he wanted. I was real scared the whole time . . . scared he'd kill me.''

Slocum turned his attention back to Moss while he spoke to the girl. "You picked some mighty bad company. And you're wrong about another thing. When I do find Jake, and I will even if it takes a month of Sundays, I'll be the one doing the killing.''

"You ain't never met nobody mean as Jake.''

Slocum chuckled mirthlessly. "He's never met up with anyone like me,'' he said, tucking the blanket under Moss's chin. "All I gotta do is find him, but that'll have to wait for a spell, until I see to my friend. Putting him on a horse will only add to his misery, and I couldn't watch him suffer any more'n he is. We'll wait here until . . .'' He could not finish saying it, even though he knew it was certain Moss would die.

"I might can tell you a way to help him,'' Pearl said in a soft voice, "only I gotta pee real bad. If you'll untie my hands so I can take down my pants, I'll show you somethin' Jake left behind over yonder where you found me.''

Slocum wagged his head. "I won't untie your hands, you little bitch. I don't trust you, which should come as no damn surprise. Stand up and I'll open your pants for you. Other-

wise you can piss in 'em for all I care. Tell me what's over
there that'll help my friend. I can go myself, but not until
I've got you tied to one of these trees."

Pearl stood up, not without difficulty with her hands tied
behind her. "There's this bottle of laudanum. Jake drank it
all the time 'cause he said it made him feel good. It's in the
saddle pocket behind that saddle he left behind. He was in
too big a hurry to saddle one of the other horses when he
heard one more rider comin', figurin' it was part of a posse
from Fort Smith lookin' for us."

Slocum got up, reaching for the top button on Pearl's
pants as he said, "Laudanum would be a help." He pushed
her pants down to her knees, wary of being kicked by her.
"Walk over yonder to get rid of your water. Then you're
coming with me to show me where the laudanum is."

She wasn't wearing any undergarments, Slocum saw as
she stepped out of her britches without a word. Her bare
white ass gleamed in the moonlight when she walked a few
steps to a nearby bush and squatted down. Seeing her naked
buttocks reminded Slocum of the night he'd spent with her
in Fort Smith, a night that had begun with bliss and ended
with treachery.

Pearl stood a moment later and started down to the river,
leaving her pants behind on the rock. "I'll show you where
it's at," she said, entering the shallows. "It's a little purple
bottle wrapped in a rag. Best I recall, there's about half of
it left. Jake mixed it with whiskey, an' that's when he got
meaner'n usual. Sometimes he grinned while he was whup-
pin' me, an' I knowed there was somethin' wrong inside his
head."

Slocum entered the water behind her, watching her slender legs navigate the uneven bottom. They came out on the

far side and turned west until they came to the spot where he'd found her.

"In that left saddle pocket," she said, unable to point to it with her hands behind her. "There's some buffalo jerky in there too, wrapped in a piece of oilskin."

Slocum knelt beside the saddle, mildly disappointed when he discovered it was not his expensive shop-made Traveler, to begin digging in the saddlebag for the laudanum, and food that might come in handy between there and Kansas City. He found the bottle and oilskin. As he was standing up he saw something else, a pleasant find. His stovepipe boots lay next to the blanket where Pearl had been sitting. Slocum wondered if Willow had located his hidden five-dollar gold piece.

To his surprise, he felt the tiny coin still sewn in place in the lining of a boot top. "At least now I'm five dollars richer than I was," he muttered, taking both boots along with the rest of the bounty.

With the girl in front of him they re-crossed the Marias, and he went to Moss's side, uncorking the little bottle of laudanum. "You gotta wake up long enough to swallow this, pardner," he said as he shook Moss's shoulder. "It'll help ease your pain a little bit."

The old man opened his eyes, taking the bottle between his trembling lips. He swallowed, shuddering. "I'm . . . cold," he said in a hollow, almost soundless whisper. His gaze became fixed on Slocum's face. "Don't let . . . me die . . . like this. I'm . . . beggin' you. Put a bullet . . . through my skull . . . like you would . . . a horse with . . . a broke leg. Don't . . . let . . . me suffer."

In spite of all he'd seen during the war and since, Slocum's eyes misted. "I can't do that, pardner, not to a friend. It ain't the same."

"Then . . . gimme a gun. I'll . . . do it . . . myself."

Hearing Moss's request was like a knife through Slocum's heart. "Don't ask me to do that either. This laudanum will be enough to keep you from suffering so much."

Moss blinked. "We both know . . . I'm gonna die. Promise me. You'll . . . let me end it . . . my own way. All you gotta do . . . is lay a gun down . . . beside me."

"It'd be the same as killing you myself. There's a slim chance you'll recover. I've seen it before. I'll stay right here till it's over, or until you're better, but don't ask me to put a gun in your hand. I just can't do it."

Moss took a deep breath and closed his eyes, slipping back into unconsciousness.

"Damn," Slocum whispered, looking up at the stars through a veil of tears. He spoke to Moss even though his friend couldn't hear him now. "I'll promise you one thing, pardner. I'll find Cut Face Jake Willow, and when I do he'll wish he was dead a thousand times before I end it."

Pearl stirred, shifting her weight to the other foot where she stood beside the river. "Jake's headed for Kansas City, a place called Diamond Lil's near the stockyards. He's got some friends there."

Slocum turned to her, fingering water from his eyelids as he spoke. "I don't give a damn if he crosses the border into Canada because I'll be right behind him."

"I'll help you find him if you'll turn me loose, Mr. Slocum. I want him dead bad as you do. Look at what he done to my face. I can take you to Diamond Lil's, 'cause I been there before, when my man worked the card tables. Jake's gonna sell that knife in Kansas City too, an' prob'ly your bay stallion. He'll get on a drunk that'll last for days, an' that's when it'll be easier to kill him."

"I'm not turning you loose," he said, spitting out the

words as though they had a bad taste. "Now sit down on that fucking rock while I think. I can't let my old friend suffer and I can't give him a gun so he can shoot himself, so just shut the fuck up while I figure out what to do!"

Pearl drew back from his sudden outburst, seating herself on the rock beside her pants. "I was only offerin' to help," she said, tucking her bare knees under her chin.

"You've been enough help already. I'm here because of you, watching a good man die from a bullet that was intended for me, so don't offer me any more of your goddamn help. I don't need it and I damn sure don't want it."

"Sorry, Mr. Slocum," she whispered. "Maybe you don't know what it's like, bein' a woman all alone without no money or even a friend who cares about you. My pa died when I was six an' my mama run off with this drummer when I was thirteen. She told me if I needed money to sell some of my charms, if you know what I mean, only I never done that. Not exactly. When Dan came along he made me big promises, that we'd go plumb to California an' see all the sights. He wasn't nothin' but a liar an' a thief, just like Jake. I ain't had all that much good luck when it comes to findin' a man."

A part of Slocum wanted to believe her, while another part warned him to be careful, to remember that Pearl was clever, just clever enough to talk him into dropping his guard so she could steal a horse and get away. Hers was a sad story, if it was the truth, which he found himself seriously doubting.

"Shut up so I can think," he said again, distracted when Moss began to shiver in his sleep. He touched the old man's shoulder gently and heard him groan, his face twisting in pain despite being unconscious. "I can't hardly stand to watch any more of this, of what's happening to him, but there ain't a damn thing I can do about it."

Pearl cleared her throat. "You could do like he asked, give him a gun so he won't hurt no more."

He glared at her. "When I want your advice I'll ask for it. In the meantime, keep your damn mouth shut."

She lowered her head, looking down at her bare feet.

Slocum's torment only worsened as the night hours passed and he heard Moss groaning. Pearl appeared to be asleep, resting her head on her pants, covered with a second thin blanket Slocum had taken from Moss's bedroll. Slocum sipped bitter corn whiskey and stared up at the sky, thinking, remembering, wondering what to do. He was faced with a choice no man wanted, to end a friend's suffering by ending his life, or allow him to die slowly and painfully from his wound.

"It just ain't fair," he whispered into a gentle night wind blowing from the northwest. "Lady Luck smiles on some and shits on the rest."

Pearl sat up, hearing his quiet voice. "I know what you must be feelin' right now."

He turned his gaze her way. "It's on account of you and that sorry-ass halfbreed I'm in this fix. The yellow son of a bitch hasn't got the balls to face me like a man, so he ambushes my pardner instead."

"I said I was sorry an' that Jake made me do it, robbin' you like I done."

"Save your apologies. It's too goddamn late for 'em in the first place. The damage is done."

"You ain't gonna believe this now, but I really did like you when we met in your room. You was 'bout the nicest man I ever met in my whole life."

"You're right. I don't believe you." He glanced down at Moss, then to the horizon. "It'll be light soon. I don't figure Willow will be coming back, so I can build a fire, make a little coffee, and maybe some soup from that jerky. Moss has some coffee beans in his gear, and a little pot to boil it in."

"I can help, if you'll untie my hands."

"I don't intend to untie your hands until we get to the marshal's office in Kansas City."

"You're gonna put me in jail?"

"It's where you belong. You're a thief, and after what just happened to my pardner, you could be charged with taking part in a murder."

"I didn't shoot him. Please, Mr. Slocum. You gotta believe me when I tell you I didn't want no part of this, that Jake made me do it."

"You'll have a chance to tell it to a judge."

Pearl started to cry, making no sound, tears rolling down her pale cheeks. "Was you ever all alone, Mr. Slocum, with nobody to look out for you?"

"I had a good family back in Georgia. I was on my own when I went off to war."

"Then you couldn't never understand what it's like to be a girl out on her own at thirteen, without a cent to my name after my ma ran off."

"Can't say as I could, but it's no excuse to take up robbery and murder. There's honest ways to make a living." He found he was uncomfortable now, hearing the plea in Pearl's voice. Was he getting soft on her in spite of everything that had happened?

He took another swallow of whiskey and stood up. "I'll get a fire started," he said. "Stay put or there'll be hell to pay."

16

"That medicine's helpin' him sleep," Pearl said after she took a look at Moss. A mid-morning sun put a glare on the water behind her.

Slocum had put a bandage around Moss's wound after sunrise, a piece of the old man's spare shirt. He blew steam from a tin cup of weak coffee laced with whiskey. "He's breathing slower now. Maybe it won't be long until..." He didn't finish.

"If you'll take off this rope I could sure use a bath in the river," she said. "Jake wouldn't let me have time to wash myself off, him worryin' you was a posse."

"I don't suppose it would hurt. You won't run far in bare feet without any clothes." He got up and came over behind her to unfasten a short length of sisal binding her wrists. Her wrists were bleeding where the rope had cut into her flesh.

When his hands were free she stood up, keeping her back to him as if out of modesty. She tiptoed into the shallows, and he couldn't help admiring her perfect figure, a tiny waist and well-rounded buttocks, the curve of her thighs. It had been too dark in his hotel room to see that much of her body. In brilliant sunlight he could see every detail.

"Too bad you had to turn out to be a thief," he told her as she waded deeper. "You're a pretty thing, but I suppose poison can come in a pretty package."

When water touched the tops of her thighs, she sank down to her chin, shivering once when cold water gave her a chill. "You never will believe I didn't *want* to do it, that Jake made me," she said, scrubbing herself with either palm.

"Nope. I'm a mighty hard man to convince when it comes to stealing. You could have left him if he wanted you to do something you objected to."

"He'd only have found me an' beat hell outa me when he did," she said. "I took up with him after Dan ran off, an' Jake figured I was his property."

He watched her stand up, her ripe young body glistening with a coating of water. She turned so he could see her breasts, and her rosy nipples twisted into hard little knots. The golden hair at the tops of her thighs resembled the fuzz on a late-spring peach. In spite of himself he felt his cock swelling with desire, and he looked away quickly, to keep the urge from making him think of doing a foolish thing.

"I seen you starin' at me," she said, smiling as she came toward him out of the river.

"I was remembering what it was like to be with you before I found out you were a thief," he said. "I said you were pretty, but not near pretty enough to take chances with again."

She came out of the water to stand on the flat rock with the front of her body turned in his direction. "You was a real good lover, Mr. Slocum. The gentle kind, only you have a big prick an' it sure felt good, even if it did hurt a little."

"Put your shirt on. I'm tying your hands again. Don't think for a minute I'll ever trust you."

She bent down to pick up her shirt, breasts swaying slightly on her rib cage. "Please don't tie that rope so tight. I got cuts where it used to be. See here?" She extended both arms to show him her rope marks.

"It'll be tight enough so you can't work it loose," he said without turning around to look at her.

"I like bein' tied up gentle when it's on a bed," she said playfully. "Sometimes it can be good when a man's rough, just so he ain't too rough."

"Put the shirt on and shut up," he snapped, seeing through her thinly disguised plan to lure him between her thighs. He picked up the rope and bound her hands behind her back, snug but not as tightly as before.

She sat on the rock with her knees parted so that, if he were to look, he had a glimpse of her silken cunt. However, he didn't look but once, turning back to Moss, then to the skyline to the north. "Willow's getting farther away with every hour," he said bitterly.

"I told you where to find him when we get to Kansas City," the girl replied. "I know you don't believe me, but I'm gonna do everythin' I can to help you get your money an' that knife back, so you'll know I ain't as wicked as you think. You got good reason to hate what I done to you. I understand how it looks. But just you wait an' see. When we get to Kansas City I'm gonna take you straight to him, if we don't stay here too long waitin' for your friend to die."

"We're staying until it's over, one way or another," Slocum said.

Later, Moss groaned again in his deep slumber, and the sound made Slocum's inner pain that much worse. And he felt tired after a night without sleep, his senses dulled by fatigue. He knew he would have to tie the girl to a tree trunk in order to get some sleep tonight . . . if Dale Moss held onto his life that much longer.

The wind picked up, driving dust from the hills around them in powdery clouds. Slocum settled in for a long day, with the knowledge that to Moss, the day would seem even longer, like an eternity, while enduring so much pain.

Full dark blanketed the prairie. Slocum could barely keep his eyes open. Moss had a fever now, and he muttered in his sleep about apparently senseless things—a woman named Louise, someone else he called Chubby. His skin felt hot to the touch, and a few times Slocum took a cloth to the river to soak it and wipe down the old man's forehead and cheeks.

Pearl tried to talk to Slocum several times during the afternoon, and he always silenced her with a look. She sat staring at the water, bare from the waist down, refusing any of the soup he made from river water and salty jerky.

As the North Star beamed bright from the heavens, Slocum got up wearily. "I'm gonna tie you to that tree yonder so I can get some sleep," he told Pearl.

"If you just tie my feet I can lay down," she protested. "I can't sleep settin' up against a tree. I sure can't go nowhere with my ankles tied. I'll lay right here in this blanket till you wake up, an' that way I won't be so awful cold."

He gave in, nodding to her, taking the second length of rope to bind her ankles, using great care not to look at her bare cunt while he did so, even though it was exposed right before his eyes. He covered her with the blanket after she curled into a ball with her head resting on her folded britches.

"G'night, Mr. Slocum," she said quietly. "I sure am sorry I brung you all this grief."

"Don't try anything dumb," he said as he found a place in the grass across from her, resting his head on a saddle blanket with his pistol clamped in his right fist. "I'm a real light sleeper."

He closed his eyes and was immediately in a sound sleep.

Something warm and wet against his cock awakened him with a start. He jerked his head off the saddle blanket to see if he might be dreaming, and right at first, in the dark, he only saw a shape bending over his crotch. With lightning-fast reactions he swung his .44 toward the figure and almost pulled the trigger, until he recognized Pearl . . . and what she was doing. With her hands still tied behind her back, her ankles bound together, she had somehow inched across the grass and opened his pants while he was in a deep sleep. Only the wet flicking of her tongue along the length of his shaft had pierced his exhausted slumber.

"What the hell?" he asked sleepily. "How did you get over here?"

She smiled up at him. "I crawled. Had to turn around so I was backwards to open them fasteners on your britches, an' I was real careful too, 'cause I was scared you'd wake up an' shoot me dead before I could do what I wanted." She curled her tongue across his glans. "I coulda grabbed your gun if I'd wanted to, only I didn't. Now lie still, Mr. Slocum, an' I'll make you feel real good. I know I done you wrong on account of Jake, but I'm gonna try an' make it up to you."

He lowered the gun to his side. He didn't want this from Pearl, not now, not after all she'd put him through, but with his cock throbbing, engorged with blood, it was hard to make the word "no" come from his throat.

She opened her mouth and took his cock between her lips

as her tongue went to work gently back and forth, up and down, then curling, licking him while she sucked his member, bobbing her head up and down slowly. A tingling sensation began in the end of his prick, spreading down his shaft to his balls.

The muscles in his buttocks tightened. His cock grew harder and thicker. Pearl increased the slow tempo of her sucking and licking. Her warm saliva ran down his prick, mingling with his pubic hair.

He gave up all thoughts of resistance when his testicles rose higher in his scrotum, ready to explode. In the back of his mind he knew he should be forcing her to stop. He promised himself he would not let this change his mind about her, about turning her over to the law in Kansas City. She had been a party to a crime, a robbery, and no amount of pleasure she might give him would turn him aside from that objective.

When the intensity of his desire reached a peak he could no longer ignore, he stiffened. A flood of jism spouted from the head of his cock in rhythmic waves, spurts of his juices accompanied by sheer ecstasy. Pearl's cheeks bulged, and yet she kept on sucking, bobbing her head, moaning softly when her mouth filled, cum spilling from her tightly compressed lips, too much for her to contain in a single mouthful.

Slocum sank back on the grass when his balls emptied, and for a moment he lay there gasping while Pearl continued to suck him dry. Finally she stopped, lifting her head, smiling at him in the moonlight.

"Don't you feel better now?" she whispered. She glanced down at his cock before he answered. "If you'll untie my feet I'll make you feel even better. You're still hard. I promise you I won't run away."

"I don't think . . . ." he began as she sat back and swung her legs around so her ankles were within easy reach.

"Just untie me, please," she begged. "I want you to make me feel good too."

He placed his pistol behind his head on the saddle blanket and unfastened the ropes binding her feet together. He still had a weakening notion to stop her. "This won't change my mind about a goddamn thing when it comes to you," he warned, just as her ankle ropes fell away, "and I damn sure won't untie your hands so you can make a grab for my gun."

She lifted one shapely leg over him so that her mound was positioned directly above his cock. "This is the only thing I mean to grab," she said thickly, gazing down at his member with a look of fascination on her face.

She lowered herself slightly, until the wet lips of her cunt touched the head of his cock. "I don't see how it can still be so hard," she said, her breathing quickening. "You ain't like most men that way."

Now Pearl pushed her weight down, spreading her cunt over him, maneuvering her body and his prick without the use of her hands until the tip of his cock was inside her. "Oh, that feels good." She sighed, closing her eyes briefly, a tiny shiver of delight running down her thighs.

"You're all wet," he said, watching her, giving in to the moment.

"It gets me all excited to suck a great big dick like the one you got," she said, pressing downward with more weight even when there was stiff resistance. "You come more'n most men do, the ones I've knowed, but it still stays hard as a rock. Dan's went limp right away, right after. Jake got so drunk that sometimes it wouldn't get hard at all. He'd beat me up an' say it was my fault, 'cause I wasn't pretty enough.''

"You're pretty enough," Slocum told her, feeling that good sensation return to his prick.

Pearl raised her cunt and then lowered it sharply, pushing more of his prick into her depths. "That feels so damn good," she said. "It hurts some, but it ain't nearly so bad I'd want to stop."

He reached for her shirt and opened the buttons that were not torn off, peeling it over her shoulders, giving him an unobstructed view of her breasts. He took a nipple in each hand and twisted it with his fingers and thumbs, pinching them lightly as he rolled them back and forth.

"Harder," she hissed. "Mash 'em a little harder, 'cause it makes 'em feel so good."

He granted her simple request, putting more pressure between his fingertips.

"Oh, yes!" she groaned, and suddenly she hunched downward to the base of his shaft with all her strength and weight. She made as if to scream, until she glanced over at Moss. Then she began thrusting up and down on his cock with her mouth tightly closed.

Soon, beads of sweat formed on her forehead and between her bobbing breasts. She drove herself against him with ever-increasing fury, slamming her pelvis into him harder and harder.

They reached a powerful climax at the same time, her body so rigid her chest felt like it was cast from iron. He spewed his jism into her cunt, arching his spine, thrusting until the last of his seed was spent.

He heard her gasping as soon as her body slackened, and he also needed a moment to catch his breath. He stared up at her, wondering if he could really put this girl in jail after all.

17

He and Pearl were in the river bathing, ridding themselves of the aftermath of their lust, when Slocum heard a sound that sent him whirling toward the bank . . . the muffled explosion of a gunshot.

"No!" he cried, stumbling headlong through the shallows to reach Dale Moss. Before he got there he knew he was too late, and that the responsibility was his, for he'd left his pistol on the saddle blanket long enough to wash himself, keeping the girl close beside him so she couldn't betray him.

In dawn's early light he found what he'd expected to see, as Pearl raced up beside him. Moss lay on his side with the pistol still in his mouth, fragments of brain and skull and tufts of hair spread over the grass above what was left of his head. A spray of dark blood colored everything around the spot where he lay, crimson droplets still clinging to blades of dry grass and one edge of the saddle blanket.

Slocum sank to his knees next to the old scout, tears in his eyes that were beyond his control. He wept silently, the way he had when he'd found his brother Robert at Gettysburg.

"No," he said again, quietly this time. "I reckon he just

couldn't take any more of the pain. If I hadn't left the gun right there where he could reach it . . .''

Pearl stood off to one side without her clothes on. She made no effort to cover herself as she stared at the body. "He did what he figured he had to do, Mr. Slocum," she said. "Won't do no good to blame yourself. He musta been hurtin' awful bad."

"I'm sure he was," Slocum answered dully, overcome by grief. He told himself that this was what Moss had wanted, an end to the pain, a way to die without lingering. "He was as brave a man as I ever knew back during the Apache campaigns. He wasn't scared of no man on earth. It wasn't for lack of courage he did this to himself. It took guts to pull that trigger, knowing it was the last thing he'd do in this lifetime. He was a tough old cuss, but I guess he knew this was one fight he couldn't win."

"Jake's the one who done this," she said. "If we ride hard I bet we can catch him at Diamond Lil's. But I'll tell you this 'bout Jake . . . he won't let you take him alive. You'll *have* to kill him, 'less he kills you first. You'd better be real smart if you aim to get him, an' you'd damn sure better be good with a gun."

Slocum gently removed his Colt .44 from Moss's frozen fingers and stood up. "I reckon I'm a little of both. First, I'm gonna bury my friend and mark his grave. Then we're headed to Kansas City, to this place called Diamond Lil's. We'll see who's the smartest and who's the best shot, just as soon as I set eyes on Willow."

Very slowly, Slocum turned north, slitting his eyes when he looked at the horizon. "Cut Face Jake has an appointment with his personal executioner, only I don't figure he's smart enough to know it yet. But I swear on Dale Moss's fresh grave he will soon enough. Get dressed, and get ready to do a hell of a lot of hard riding.''

He stood with his head bowed above a shallow grave he'd dug with a willow branch. It was covered with stones to keep wolves and coyotes from digging up Moss's remains. The grave was on a cut bank above the Marias River, and Slocum knew the next big spring flood would wash it away. However, he figured it wouldn't matter to Moss, and the old Indian scout would probably just as soon have his bones scattered across an open prairie somewhere in Kansas as buried underground.

He turned to Pearl where she was holding the horses. He hadn't tied her hands again. ''Let's ride,'' he said, climbing aboard the buttermilk gelding, waiting for her to step up on the Palouse. ''I'm gonna leave your hands free, but if you think you can double-cross me, you'll find out just how wrong you are. You got lucky the first time, but only a damn fool counts on luck. Don't test me.''

She reined her horse toward the river. ''You're gonna find out you was dead wrong about me,'' she said, urging the Palouse downslope. ''I robbed you an' there ain't no denyin' it, but I had a reason. Jake hit me so hard I lost track of the times, an' I was scared he'd kill me if I didn't do like he said. But if you'll trust me just a little, I'll take you right to where he is. Only, I sure hope you're as good as you say with that gun.''

They crossed the river at a trot, and struck a lope on the far side heading north.

Just once, Slocum turned back in the saddle for a last look at Dale Moss's final resting place. His throat became tight, and he fixed his attention on the road that would take them to Kansas City. He judged they were little more than a hard day's ride away and if their horses held up, they should make it after dark, probably well before midnight.

It had become a major city in the West built on beef. Miles of stockyards had been erected along railroad tracks and sidings. Kansas City slaughterhouses were in competition with Chicago's to provide eastern states with meat. Thousands of bawling longhorns and newer crossbreds awaited butchering in feed yards designed to put more fat on cattle carcasses. Cattle buyers had offices at the yards, buying and selling, trading lesser animals for better grades in hopes of landing more profitable contracts with packing plants. Slocum remembered it as a rough town in spots, full of con men and card cheats and undesirable types, and the usual cowboys who filled railroad cattle cars with their herds and then accompanied them to the end of the line to see the sights: fine hotels, gambling houses, and stores of every description where a cowhand could spend what little hard-earned money he had.

Slocum and Pearl arrived at the outskirts of Kansas City at a quarter past ten that evening, pushing tired horses to the limit over a distance of almost fifty miles. Beyond endless rows of cattle pens, the lights from a saloon district beckoned to men who were thirsty, looking for a card game, or looking for a woman for hire at the right price.

All day Slocum had been remembering Dale Moss: their time at Fort Grant, quiet nights around campfires, close scrapes with Apache war parties, how Moss seemed to be able to track a butterfly across a frozen lake in winter or solid rock in Arizona Territory's blistering summer heat in the Dragoon Mountains. He didn't want to recall those times, not with Moss lying in a grave behind them. But the memories kept returning.

"Diamond Lil's is way over yonder," Pearl said, pointing to the saloon district. "There's an alley runs behind it. My man used to run out that back door plenty of times when he got caught cheatin' at cards. He wasn't no better cheatin' at cards than he was lovin' a woman."

Slocum wasn't paying much attention to what she said, his gaze fixed on streets lined with false-fronted drinking parlors, a few of them two-story affairs with upstairs rooms for prostitutes and opium dens. Just about anything money could buy was offered for sale in Kansas City, he knew, although he hadn't been there often, preferring open spaces out west to crowded cities.

"First thing we're gonna do is find the local law," he told her.

She looked down at her hands resting on the saddlehorn for a moment. "Then you're gonna put me in jail, I reckon," she said.

"Depends," he replied, guiding his horse between corrals full of cattle. "I'm gonna tell the law why I'm here, and about Jake Willow, to see if I can get this done legal. But if I don't get cooperation from them, I'll handle it my own way."

"You said it depends, havin' me put in jail," Pearl continued. "Depends on what?"

"On how good the information you give me turns out to be. If Jake's at Diamond Lil's like you say he is, I'll let you go. But if he ain't, if it's just another one of your damn lies, I swear you'll pay for it with a stay behind bars."

"He's there," Pearl promised. "He said he was gonna show that gold-handled knife to a guy named Sloan. Sloan buys all kinds of stolen stuff, for half what it's really worth. My man used to sell him gold watches he took off drunks. Dan was a pickpocket too, only he weren't much good at that neither. He got caught when we was up in Saint Louis an' spent a whole month in jail 'cause he took a gold ring off this fella one time. The fella went to the law an' had Dan arrested before he could sell that ring. I woulda left Dan then, only I didn't have no money an' our ol' wagon had busted spokes.''

Slocum had made up his mind to let the girl go anyway, for as he listened to more and more of her story, she sounded more like the victim of circumstances than a criminal. But before he told her what he meant to do, he needed to get as much information as he could about Jake Willow's habits and any other details she might remember, such as his plans after he finished in Kansas City. ''Where can I find this Sloan?'' he asked as they neared three streets crowded with saloons.

''He has this little jewelry shop up on Center Street. I can show you, only I imagine he's closed for the night. Sometimes when Dan had somethin' to sell, he went round to the back an' knocked on the door even if it was late. Jake won't waste no time findin' out what that knife is worth.''

''The city marshal's office is right across from the town square, I recall, so that's where we'll stop off first.''

Pearl hung her head and didn't say any more, as if she fully expected to be jailed as soon as they got there.

He led them wide of the saloon district to ride uptown, with a few gas streetlights showing him the way. Part of Kansas City had roadways made of brick, and when their horses struck that part of town, the echo of shod hooves off houses and buildings was too loud for his liking. They passed canopied carriages rolling back and forth across the heart of the city, a few smaller buggies with open tops, and occasional horsemen, most of them dressed in fine evening attire. Cowhands mostly kept to the rough side of town near the stockyards, in Slocum's experience. Thus Slocum saw few riders in wide-brimmed hats and chaps with ropes tied to stock saddles.

At an intersection, Pearl pointed east. "Yonder's Sloan's place," she said.

A sign above a narrow brick shop read "Sloan Jewelry and Goldsmithing." The shop's front windows were dark.

"I'll come back," he said, "as soon as I've had a talk with the city marshal as to my reasons for being here." He urged the roan across the empty intersection, sighting a courthouse steeple a few blocks away.

A light was burning behind a glass-paned window with "City Marshal Wilson Young" painted on it when they reached the town square. For the most part, the streets were empty downtown. Slocum swung down, working stiffness from his knees as he tied the roan to an iron loop affixed to a porch post.

Pearl was slower to dismount, and he heard her sniffling as she tied the Palouse to a neighboring post.

"Inside," he said, not too gruffly.

She halted on the steps and turned to him, tears brimming in her eyes. "Don't let Jake kill you," she said, choking on difficult words. "I know I gotta go to jail 'cause of what I done. But don't let Jake get away with this. If there ever was a man who needed killin', it's Jake. He's just plain no good."

He took her by the arm without saying a word and escorted her into the lamplit city marshal's office.

A hard-faced man of thirty or so in a bowler hat looked up from a rolltop desk when they entered. "What can I do for you folks?" he asked, taking note of their dusty, grime-coated attire as if he'd just scented a polecat's smell.

Slocum took Pearl to a chair against one wall, then came

over to the desk. "My name's John Slocum. I'm from Denver, and I was robbed of almost a thousand dollars and a very valuable old dagger down in Fort Smith. The same man stole my horse. I've followed him here. He goes by the name Cut Face Jake Willow, and I'm told by U.S. Deputy Marshal Heck Thomas he's suspected of several killings and plenty of thefts in Kansas Territory. With the help of this girl, I now believe I know where he is, a place called Diamond Lil's over by the stockyards. I want him arrested for theft, and also for a murder he committed. He shot a friend of mine down on the Marias River. We just buried him this morning."

The man in the bowler merely shrugged. "The crimes you say were committed are out of my jurisdiction, Mr. Slocum. You can take your complaint to the U.S. marshal's office tomorrow, only I can tell you now that without witnesses, about all Marshal Cox can do is wait until proper warrants come from down in Fort Smith. He'll have to verify everything you just told me and wait for a legal warrant. He can't just up an' arrest some fellow based on your say-so, and neither can I." He chuckled. "You don't look like the kind of man who'd carry almost a thousand dollars. I'm afraid I find your story hard to believe, but if you can convince a judge down in Fort Smith to issue a warrant, Marshal Cox will put him in jail."

Slocum spoke evenly. "That'll be too late. By then Willow will have sold the dagger and my horse, and probably spend a lot of my money."

Another shrug from the city marshal. "Tell it to Marshal Jim Cox tomorrow morning. If you can convince him you're telling the truth, maybe he'll look into it."

Slocum turned away from the desk. "You aren't leaving

me any choice,'' he said. Then he spoke to Pearl. ''C'mon
with me. I want you to show me the livery stable where
Willow's most likely to put horses. Then we've got a stop
to make at a jewelry shop.''

18

Brown's Livery was quiet, appearing deserted until a candle was lit in a tiny room with a single window off to one side of the barn. A man dressed in long underwear peered out to see who had ridden horses to the stable door.

"We need to put up two horses for the night," Slocum said, "and we're looking for a friend, a guy with a scar on his face who has a big bay Thoroughbred stud."

"He was here. Paid cash money in advance. Said to keep an eye on that stud an' two more, a black an' a sorrel. Seems he did have a big scar on his cheek. You've come to the right place tonight, mister."

Slocum got down off the roan. "I was thinking of making an offer on that stud. Mind if I get a look at him while we're putting these horses away?"

"Don't reckon it'll hurt. Pull yer saddles an' follow me. Got two stalls at the back."

Slocum quickly stripped Moss's saddle off the roan, and then helped Pearl get the saddle off the Palouse. "Don't say a word," he warned her, leaving Moss's Sharps rifle booted to the saddle.

The liveryman lit a lantern and turned up the wick as they

led both horses down an alleyway between stalls. Right off, Slocum saw his stud in a stall to the right. He stopped at the gate to look inside.

What he saw made his belly roll. His bay had bloody gashes along its ribs where spurs had dug into its flesh. He clamped his jaw shut, then followed the stable keeper to put the roan and the Palouse away, paying for their keep with his five-dollar coin, waiting while his change was counted out.

"Looks like he used that stud mighty rough," Slocum said, pocketing what the stable keeper gave him, finding he was unable to remain totally silent about the abuse given his bay. "Those are deep cuts on its sides."

"Some men ain't got no horse sense. Feller acted half drunk to me, kinda wobbly-legged, stinkin' of whiskey. But he paid fer stalls with cash money, an' he didn't ask what I thought of them spur marks. It's his animal, so I reckon he can treat it just about any way he chooses."

Slocum didn't say anything, walking out of the barn with Pearl beside him, carrying his Winchester beside his leg. When he found Willow, *if* he found him tonight, there would probably be close-quarters fighting and the rifle would be useless. But it was a creed with Slocum to be prepared for anything, and as a result he brought the Winchester along just in case.

"Show me Diamond Lil's," he said, guiding Pearl toward the rows of saloons. Even from a distance they could hear music and laughter coming from the district above the incessant bawling of cattle in the shipping pens.

"It's got two floors," she said. "You can see it right yonder, the one with the flat roof. The street's called Drover's Avenue, an' there's an alley behind it. If I was you I'd go in the back way up them stairs to the second floor.

Jake'll be watchin' the front, or he'll have somebody watchin' it for him. You can come downstairs from the inside. There's this big staircase leadin' up to the whores' rooms. He won't be expectin' nobody to come from up there. In case you wasn't listenin', the old man at the stable said Jake acted drunk.''

"I was listening real close," Slocum whispered savagely as his rage became like a red-hot coal under a blacksmith's bellows, growing hotter as they neared Diamond Lil's and the man who had cost him so much over the past few difficult days. Now it was more than money and a dagger and a horse he sought. Vengeance gripped him, a desperate, seething need for revenge for what had happened to an old, dear friend. "Drunk or sober, it don't make any difference to me," he added quietly. "He's gonna be just as dead either way."

They stepped across the last railroad siding, very near the saloon lights, leaving the total darkness behind them. Slocum saw Diamond Lil's, half a block up a street where clusters of drinking parlors and gambling houses lined the boardwalks. Dozens of horses were tied to posts and hitch rails along Drover's Avenue. He caught a glimpse of the alleyway Pearl had told him about, and when he did, he reached for her arm to halt her. "You've shown me all I need to see," he said. "I may be making a mistake, but I've decided to trust you. Go back to the livery and saddle Moss's white-rumped horse." He reached into a pocket, handing her three dollars in currency. "This won't get you far, but it'll get you out of town and buy you something to eat. If you've told me the truth, I'm gonna square things with Willow tonight. If you haven't, if it's all a lie, then you can brand me a fool a second time."

She shook her head, refusing his money. "I'm stayin' till

it's over. I wanna see Jake dead 'cause of the way he treated me an' what he made me do. If he kills you, I'll take the horse an' clear out, but I don't want no more of your money an' I ain't leavin' till I see how it ends.''

"You won't be safe if he sees you first, and he'll know someone brought you here. I want you out of the way when the shooting starts."

"I'll stay hid right close to the stable, out behind the barn someplace. If I see you come for your horse, I'll know you got him. If I see Jake, I'll stay hid till he rides out of town on your bay. I'll tell that U.S. marshal what happened, how he robbed you an' all. I'll even admit what I done to help him, but I ain't leavin' town till I know."

He stuffed the currency into the waistband of her pants, for it was all he had to give her. "Wait at the livery then. Can't say exactly why, but I believe you. Stay out of sight. If I don't make it back, you've got my gratitude for taking me this far. Now get going."

Pearl stood on her tiptoes and kissed him lightly on the cheek, then turned and ran off into the darkness, heading back in the direction of the stable without another word.

Slocum angled toward the alley, being as careful as he could to avoid being seen, especially carrying a rifle. This part of Kansas City would be no different than any other cow town, with deputy marshals likely to be patrolling the area in case trouble broke out, which it often did when tough men and whiskey got together. He couldn't afford any delays, any explanations as to why he'd brought a Winchester to the saloon district, and his appearance was such, covered with dirt and sweat stains from so many days in open country, that a peace officer was unlikely to be swayed by his story if one of them discovered him. Dressed in buckskins and moccasins, hatless and currently without a cent to his name, he could easily be mistaken for a saddle tramp or a thief on the lookout for easy pickings. Thus he hid himself as best he could, crossing over to the mouth of the alley quickly until he was in deep shadows between buildings. The smells of garbage and urine from the saloons' latrines assailed his nostrils while he made his way carefully, slowly, toward the rear of Diamond Lil's.

He froze against a building when he heard a noise, and as his eyes adjusted to the blackness, he found its source farther up the alley. A drunken cowboy was relieving himself behind one of the saloons, leaning against a wall while his water splattered into a muddy latrine ditch. Slocum heard the man mumbling to himself, and couldn't quite make out the words. A moment later the cowboy turned and went back inside a rear door, briefly shedding a square of light from the opening onto the ground where he'd been standing.

Slocum proceeded more cautiously, a few feet at a time, with an ear cocked for the slightest sound. Dank smells grew worse as he came closer to the back of Diamond Lil's.

He found a back door, bolted from inside, and a set of old wood stairs leading to the second floor just as Pearl had said they would. Inside, he could hear an out-of-tune piano and a banjo accompanying a squeaky woman's voice in a song he didn't recognize.

Making his way carefully up the stairs, he watched dark rear windows closely and saw no one looking out. When he came to the top of the stairway, he tried the doorknob and found it locked, but as thin as the door was, he was sure he could shoulder through . . . although he could only guess what awaited him inside the moment he made any noise. He readied himself, taking the hammer thong off his Colt, then taking a deep breath. In the next few minutes he hoped to face the culmination of a long manhunt, the moment he'd

been heading toward over so many rugged miles of hardship
. . . and death, the death of a friend.

Bunching his chest and shoulder muscles, he threw all his
weight against the door. Wood splintered around the lock
plate and the door swung inward.

He crouched for a moment in the opening with his pistol
in his fist, looking down a dark hallway, finding it empty.
Would the noise bring someone? He tensed for the moment
when trouble started.

Laughter and music came from the far end of the hall,
and a glow came from lanterns downstairs. Five doors lined
either side of the hallway. His nose picked up a familiar
scent, the smell of opium pipes that was so common in the
dens of San Francisco. He thought he saw a faint light coming from beneath one door midway to the stairwell leading
to the ground floor. On the balls of his feet he hurried toward it, for in the same instant he heard a young woman's
voice inside calling, "Who's there?"

He found the door above the beam of light unlocked, and
with the gun aimed, he pushed the door open. A naked girl
lay on a four-poster bed with a bare-assed cowboy between
her thighs, a small lantern burning on a washstand near the
bed.

The dark-haired girl gasped.

The cowboy glanced over his shoulder, and he immediately saw Slocum's guns, a pistol aimed at him and a rifle
dangling at Slocum's side.

"What the hell?"

Slocum lowered his pistol when he got a good look at the
cowboy's face—he had no scars. Slocum spoke to the
woman. "I need to know if there's a guy downstairs with
a big scar on his face. They call him Cut Face. He's a halfbreed."

It was the young cowboy who answered. "Yeah, he's down there at the bar buyin' everybody drinks. How come you busted in our room like this on account of lookin' for him? He's standin' down yonder in plain sight."

Slocum gave him a humorless grin. "You'll probably hear the explanation in a minute or two. If you aim to stay healthy, keep on riding the woman and don't come out of this room. The climate ain't gonna be safe downstairs for folks who're looking to keep on breathing regular."

He backed out of the room and closed the door, making his way to the top of the stairs. A chorus of voices and a badly played song rose from a smoky barroom below. No one seemed to notice him or his guns. The customers were otherwise occupied with whiskey and beer and saloon girls.

Half-a-dozen men were crowded around a single individual at the bar, a coppery-skinned man with waist-length black hair tied in a braid, square shoulders, and a pair of pistols worn around his middle. He had a prominent nose, somewhat flattened at the tip, and was resting one elbow on the bar, talking animatedly to one of the men standing close.

"Willow," Slocum whispered, at long last getting a look at the man he'd been after. He didn't need to see a scar to know who he was.

He cocked his rifle, a shell already in the firing chamber, and leveled both guns on the room. Keeping his back to the wall, he started down the steps slowly, one step at a time, never taking his gaze from the face of Jake Willow. He was halfway down the stairs when a voice cried, "Hey! That feller's aimin' his guns at us!"

As Slocum expected, Willow was the first to turn, wheeling away from the bar and clawing for his pistols. Slocum took aim and fired his Colt too quickly, determined to kill his adversary at once.

The roar of his .44 was like a clap of thunder in the enclosed space, and he knew he'd aimed a fraction too low. An instant second later Willow's fists were filled with iron, and while men were yelling, diving for the floor to get out of harm's way, a pair of gunshots exploded, twin answers to Slocum's first shot.

A slug struck the wall behind him only inches from his face, while another splintered a handrail on the staircase. Slocum squeezed the Colt's trigger again just as Willow spun away to the floor as if one knee suddenly buckled.

Two more shots blasted from the confusion of piled bodies where drinkers ducked for cover. A bullet whacked into the step where Slocum was standing, another breaking glass somewhere below the stairs. He fell back, unable to take a shot at Willow for fear of harming an innocent bystander. Slocum landed on his rump, just in time to see a moving blur race for a pair of swinging doors at the front of Diamond Lil's.

"You lucky bastard!" Slocum roared, lunging to his feet, bounding down the stairs filled with rage so intense he ignored all caution when he came to the bat-wings. He ran outside, and saw a limping figure disappear between two saloons on the far side of Drover's Avenue.

His jaws clamped shut, gripping both guns fiercely, he took off after Jake as fast as his feet could move, running blindly toward the spot where Willow had gone out of sight, taking little satisfaction in the knowledge that he'd put a bullet in one of Jake's legs, even if the bloodstains would mark his trail.

19

A four-foot space, dark as ink, was a death trap for a careless man running between the two buildings. Willow was wounded and he couldn't run far, making it far more likely he would wait at the back of the saloons for a close shot at Slocum. But there were times when Slocum's temper got the best of all reason, a trait he'd inherited from his father, and now he ran headlong into the dark opening without a thought for his own safety, ducking down as low as he could to make a smaller target, hell-bent on catching up to Jake no matter how much flying lead he had to face. His heart thudded inside his chest and his mouth felt dry, cottony, the taste of fear and anger becoming one. Rifle in one hand, pistol in the other, he sprinted through the black space at full speed until he neared a starlit alley. Behind him, he heard shouts, the excitement generated by an exchange of gunshots at Diamond Lil's drawing patrons of the saloon district out in the street to see who was doing the shooting.

The sudden wink of a muzzle flash accompanied the crack of a pistol shot from a dark corner of one saloon building, sending Slocum sprawling on his face, sliding along on his chest in mud from an open sewer. He fired at the flash of light with his Colt, feeling its walnut grips jump in his palm as orange flame belched from the barrel amid the concussion of igniting gunpowder. He pulled the trigger again, shooting at a spot rather than a target, hoping to put Willow back on the run, for Slocum knew he was trapped without cover between buildings, his own muzzle flashes marking the spot where he lay. Before the boom of his second shot faded he heard running feet.

He scrambled to his hands and knees, heart pounding, jumping up to run after his quarry. Racing to the corner from which the shot was fired, he saw a darting shadow dodge back and forth down the alleyway, fifty or sixty yards away.

He steadied his revolver and nudged the trigger. A blast filled the alley with sound, along with the singsong whine of a bullet wide of its mark. He'd missed again. And as Slocum took off after the running figure, Willow fired over his shoulder, three rapid bursts of gunfire, all high and wide, slugs ricochetting off wood planks at the backs of saloons.

Running, panting, keeping his eyes glued on Jake, Slocum beat out a constant rhythm with his muddy moccasins down an alley full of overflowing trash barrels and urine ditches as he closed the distance. Jake's injured leg was slowing him down just enough to shorten the gap between them quickly.

And just as quickly Willow was gone, turning again between buildings, around another corner where a possible ambush might await Slocum if he ran straight for it.

Opportunity came when another slender opening appeared to Slocum's left, barely enough room to squeeze through. He made a turn and hurried down a particularly muddy ditch, coming out on a dirt street crowded with drinkers who'd also come outside when they'd heard the exchange of gunfire.

Slocum stumbled to a halt just in time to see Jake swing up on a bay horse tied to a hitch rail in front of a saloon. Willow jerked the horse around, bending over its neck, drumming his heels into its sides as it lunged into a gallop toward the rail-yard cattle pens.

Slocum dropped his Colt into its holster and raised his Winchester to his shoulder, drawing a careful bead on what he could see of Jake's back. When the rifle sights were steady, despite his labored breathing, he feathered the trigger as gently as a mother touching an infant's chin, making sure his shot was high enough to miss the horse.

The butt plate slammed against his shoulder muscles as an earsplitting roar filled the street. The power of a heavy-bore cartridge rocked Slocum back on his heels. As flame and smoke shot from the muzzle, Slocum heard another sound he wanted to hear. A cry of pain.

Willow slumped momentarily over the running horse's neck. Then he straightened, reaching for his left shoulder while the bounding horse rounded a turn toward the stock-yards.

"Gotcha, you son of a bitch," Slocum snarled, taking off in a run, levering another shell into the Winchester's chamber as he ran past dozens of curious onlookers who pulled back when they saw him coming with a rifle.

An unexpected rush of energy gave Slocum a burst of new speed, his moccasins flying over a rutted roadway. Perhaps it was the knowledge he'd put two bullet holes in Jake Willow that urged him on. He'd wanted the halfbreed to suffer the way Moss had, the way Slocum had, moving fifty miles across a barren wasteland, wondering if he would die of thirst or starvation.

But as Slocum left the lantern-lit street, he faced another danger, the darkness. Willow could hide almost anywhere in this maze of cowpens, making him very hard to find. What Slocum needed now was a horse, for with Jake on horseback, the chase was too one-sided, even with Willow being badly wounded.

Slocum made a dash for the stable, following the railroad tracks he and Pearl had walked along before. Willow had vanished as if into thin air, but Slocum knew he was out there somewhere, bleeding, in pain, needing medical attention sooner or later. Unless Slocum had gotten lucky enough with his second shot, hitting a vital spot high on Willow's left shoulder that might cause him to slowly bleed to death or lose consciousness.

Fatigue finally forced Slocum to stop a moment to catch his breath, and that was when he heard the clatter of horseshoes off to his right among the corrals. Wheeling toward the sound, he bent into a lumbering, exhausted run, wheezing so badly he felt sure his ribs would burst.

Off to the west a voice shouted, "Hey, you! What the hell are you doin' scatterin' these cows? Slow that horse down or I'll—" A gun exploded, silencing the voice of a cowboy doing night duty watching cattle in the shipping pens.

Near total collapse from so much running, Slocum stumbled onward toward the sound of the shot, legs numbed to the point that they almost refused his commands. He glimpsed a fast-moving shadow racing alongside a corral fence, the outline of a rider bent forward on a galloping horse, too far away for any hope of getting off a clean shot.

Another voice cried, "Some guy just shot Jessie. Come quick so we can git him to a sawbones . . . he's bleedin' real bad from a hole in his head."

Willow had just claimed another victim, Slocum thought dully, pushing himself to the limit, his lungs burning from lack of air. He could not stop running, but he couldn't keep going when his legs simply wouldn't work.

He staggered to a halt beside a fence, sucking for breath like a man who'd narrowly escaped drowning. The rider kept moving to the west at an all-out gallop, getting farther and farther away.

"Got to get a horse," Slocum gasped, reeling away from the fence. "I'll find . . . that . . . son of a bitch . . . sooner or later."

Like a drunken man he stumbled toward the livery, holding his sides while still clutching his guns. It was beginning to seem that Jake Willow had nine lives. No matter how close Slocum came to cornering him, he managed to escape in the nick of time.

"He's got to be . . . the luckiest man alive," he said in a hoarse whisper. "Or the smartest." Over the years Slocum had found himself pitted against a number of truly dangerous men, and he'd always found a way to come out on top sooner or later. But Willow had him dumbfounded. How could one man be so elusive, so hard to find and kill, he wondered.

A quarter mile down the tracks he saw the roof of the livery against the skyline. He couldn't run that distance, or even manage a slow trot. It was all he could do to put one foot in front of the other at a walk.

He thought of one consolation as he stumbled closer to the stable. The little horse Willow had stolen was a short-coupled cow pony. It would be no match for Slocum's big Thoroughbred in a contest of stamina and speed, even after the hard treatment Jake had given it on the way to Kansas City.

He was two hundred yards from the livery when he heard a thundering noise, like a shot fired by cannons during the war. It came from just in back of the barn, a deep concussion that almost shook the ground under his feet.

"What the hell?" he muttered, stopping the moment he heard it, peering into the darkness for some explanation. The sound hadn't come from any ordinary gun—he was sure of it, as well as he knew weaponry.

A lantern came to life inside the stable. Old Man Brown had been jolted from his sleep by the explosion so near his tiny room at the front.

Slocum summoned the last of his strength and broke into a trot, making the rest of the distance on legs that had no feeling left.

He saw Brown standing at the rear of the stable holding his lantern aloft. Then he heard a thin woman's voice coming from somewhere in the darkness behind the barn.

"You had it comin', Jake! After what you done to me you had it comin'!"

It was Pearl's voice. Slocum had all but forgotten about her in his mad dash to bring down Willow, not remembering that she was waiting behind the livery. But what about the explosion?

He hurried up beside the liveryman. "Bring that lamp and follow me," he gasped.

Covering their progress with his rifle, Slocum led the way down a slight incline to the bottom of a dry creek bed, guided by the sound of Pearl sobbing.

When the circle of lantern light struck Pearl, Slocum also saw someone lying near her feet. He rushed toward her, seeing she had a long-barrel rifle in her hands.

"What happened?" he asked her, still out of breath.

"I got him," Pearl cried. "I shot Jake. He was tryin' to

get to the barn.'' She pointed a trembling finger downward and dropped the heavy gun with a thud.

Slocum looked down at Jake Willow before he asked, ''Where did you get the rifle?''

''It was on that saddle, the one belonged to your friend, Dale Moss. I snuck in yonder an' got it when nobody was lookin' so I'd have a way to kill him if he killed you. It was so big I nearly couldn't carry it. When I pulled the trigger it knocked me flat. But I got him, only he ain't dead yet.''

Slocum turned to Brown. ''Hand me that lantern, then go get the city marshal.''

Before Brown gave up the light he took a closer look at the body. ''Sweet Jesus, little lady. You blowed his backbone plumb through his shirt. I can see bones stickin' out. That's the feller with the scar who stabled them three horses, includin' the stud you said you wanted to buy,'' Brown said to Slocum gravely. Then he handed him the lantern handle and hurried off toward the front of the barn. ''I'll fetch a doctor too,'' he added over his shoulder as he grabbed a saddle to saddle a horse.

''No need to hurry with that doctor on my account,'' Slocum muttered.

Pearl dried her eyes just as Willow moaned. He was lying on his face in the dirt. Bits of his spinal column protruded from a massive, bloody hole in his shirt. Moss's .52-caliber buffalo gun had left a hole the size of Slocum's fist in Jake Willow's back where the slug had exited.

Slocum put the lantern down beside Jake. Willow's eyes were open, blinking furiously. Blood pooled around him, oozing from the hole in his back, a smaller bullet hole in his left shoulder, and another wound in his leg. Willow looked at the light. Then his gaze lifted to Slocum's face.

Slocum knelt so Jake could see him clearly. "Hurts, don't it?" he asked. "I'll have to hand it to you. You're a hard man to find and even harder to kill. Only now, your backbone's broke in half and you ain't gonna run no farther. You killed a friend of mine down on the Marias. He died slow, painful. That's why I'm gonna stay right here and watch you die the same way, and I won't apologize when I tell you I'm gonna enjoy it. In case you are interested, it was Pearl who shot you this last time. She showed me where to find you."

Slocum took a quick breath. "If it matters now, my name's John Slocum, and even if the girl had missed, I'd have gotten you sooner or later. You were a dead man the minute you killed my friend Dale Moss. At first, all I was after was my money, the dagger, and my stud. But when you shot my friend, you crossed the line. It was Moss's buffalo gun that busted your spine, so I reckon it could be called justice, only it won't bring my friend back."

Slocum smiled savagely. "So I'm just gonna sit here an' watch you hurt, waiting for you to die, and I hope it takes forever. Some men ain't men at all, Willow. They're just pieces of shit that look like men. That's what you are, Cut Face, a piece of shit who's getting what you deserve. I've only got one regret. I wish it'd been me who fired that last shot. Like Pearl said, you had this coming."

Willow's eyes slitted with hatred despite what must have been excruciating agony. His lips were trembling when he opened his mouth to speak. "Fuck . . . you," he groaned, fingers clawing dirt. One foot began to twitch beyond his control, the beginning of death throes.

Slocum shook his head. "You got it wrong, Jake. You're the one who's fucked. You've got a busted spine and you're bleeding to death. You can't move, you can't even crawl, and maybe in a few hours, after you've had more pain than you ever dreamed possible, you're gonna die. I'm no expert on the topic, but it looks to me like the fucking went the other way.''

20

Dr. Jedediah Collins knelt beside Jake Willow, examining his wounds by lantern light. "His spinal column has been broken at the junction of two lumbar vertebrae. He's paralyzed from the waist down and he won't live much longer. There are massive internal injuries. I can give him morphine to ease his pain, but that's all I can do. He's going to die. It's just a matter of time."

Slocum stood beside City Marshal Wilson Young as Dr. Collins made his pronouncement. Slocum wanted to say that an injection of morphine was too humane for a bastard like Willow, but he held his tongue. Before the marshal and the doctor came, he'd taken a roll of currency from Willow's pockets. Eight hundred dollars in one pocket and three hundred in another, most likely the price he'd gotten from the man named Sloan for the old dagger, since the ancient weapon wasn't on Jake now. At first light Slocum meant to get the dagger back, but tonight, feeling as drained as he'd ever felt in his life, all he wanted was a hot bath and a bed for the night.

Marshal Young looked up at Pearl. "You admit you shot him, miss?"

"I did. He forced me to rob Mr. Slocum of all his money and an old knife of some kind. He said if I didn't do it, he'd make me sorry, that he'd hurt me bad."

Slocum intervened. "This girl led me to Willow. I won't file any charges against her, and Willow was carrying two guns at the time Pearl shot him, so it's easily a case of self-defense. I have no doubt Willow would have killed her if she'd tried to stop him from running off with my horse and my money. I can get you verification of what happened down in Fort Smith if you'll wire U.S. Deputy Marshal Heck Thomas. When the robbery occurred, I gave him a complete report of the incident."

Young rubbed his chin thoughtfully. "I'll wire Fort Smith first thing in the morning to check out your story, Mr. Slocum. If Marshal Thomas verifies what you've told me, as far as I'm concerned that'll be the last of it. No charges will be filed against this woman, although I'm still a bit puzzled. By her own admission she was an accomplice to the robbery."

"An unwilling accomplice," Slocum said. "I'm convinced she never planned any of this on her own."

Dr. Collins filled a syringe with clear liquid and pushed the needle into Jake Willow's arm. Willow had been unconscious for half an hour or more by the time the marshal and the doctor had gotten there.

"That's one hell of a hole in his back," Brown, the livery owner, said quietly, standing on the far side of Willow. "I've never seen a bullet hole that big. When I heard the gun go off, I'd have swore somebody'd tossed dynamite into my barn."

"It was a Sharps buffalo gun," Slocum said. "It can drop a fifteen-hundred-pound buffalo bull at five hundred yards if the shooter knows what he's doing."

Dr. Collins stood up. "One thing's for sure. This fellow isn't going to get up. As far as I'm concerned he's clinically dead, although he's still breathin'. A wound like that can be so painful it causes a man to lose consciousness fairly soon. Not many men can take that much pain, when the spinal cord itself is severed."

"There's more than one kind of justice," Slocum muttered as he gazed down at Willow's motionless form. "A cowboy was shot in the head by this hombre as he was trying to make it here to the livery. I imagine somebody took him to the hospital by now, if he isn't dead. I didn't see it, but I heard someone else yell to another cowboy about it after Jake fired a shot."

Dr. Collins grunted and closed his medical bag. "A doctor at the hospital will attend to him if, as you say, the man who was shot isn't dead. I'll have someone hitch a horse to one of the ambulances and drive over to pick this fellow up. We can't just leave him here, although he could easily expire before an ambulance can get here. He's lost so much blood his heart will simply stop beating shortly."

"Jake ain't got a heart," Pearl said, staring down at Willow with a curious look of detachment on her face, no longer crying or showing any emotion, calmed after the initial shock of what she had done had passed.

The marshal spoke to Slocum. "Don't leave town until I've gotten an answer back from Fort Smith, Mr. Slocum. It ain't that I don't believe the two of you, but a murder's been committed an' I have to file charges or fill out a report statin' my reasons for dismissing them."

"I understand, Marshal. If you'll direct us to a good hotel with a bathhouse, we'll be there until you've cleared everything up tomorrow."

"The Darby is a nice place over on Main. Just head north

about six blocks an' you'll see it, a big brick building five stories high. Bathtubs on every floor. A maid will bring hot water up."

"Sounds good to me," Slocum replied. "I'll get some clean clothes from my gear in the stable yonder. It's tied behind my saddle, the one Willow stole from me when he stole my horse. I have one bit of unfinished business here, with a jeweler by the name of Sloan. After I see him, I'll stop by your office."

Marshal Young scowled. "What business have you got with him?"

"I have reason to believe he's the man who bought the stolen dagger from Jake Willow. I intend to give him his money back."

"Sloan ain't got a real good reputation in this town. You may have a problem if he denies buyin' stolen property. This won't be the first time I've heard he's in that sort of business, but we've never been able to prove anything on him."

"I won't have a problem," Slocum said, keeping his plans to himself. "Me and this girl will be at your office by noon, Marshal. That should be plenty of time for an answer to come from Fort Smith. And if you need any further information about what happened, or the ownership of the dagger, contact Miss Myra Belle Shirley in Fort Smith for verification. The knife was a gift meant for her, sent by a man in Springfield, Mr. Bradford Thomas."

"I'll check on it," Young said as Slocum took Pearl by the arm, walking slowly into the dark stable to get his gear from the back of his saddle and his boots.

"This is somewhat irregular," the woman said as she placed two steaming buckets of water on the floor between two bathtubs at the Darby Hotel. "We have separate bathrooms for women at the far end of the hall."

Slocum pulled off his shirt while Pearl turned her back to the hotel maid. He reached in a pocket and handed the woman an extra pair of dollar bills. "This oughta help make it seem less irregular," he told her. "Two more buckets of hot water should be enough. Then you can leave us alone."

She took the money and left the bathroom. Pearl added the hot water to the cast-iron tubs, which were already almost half full, steam rising invitingly from both of them. Slocum began soaping his face to shave off several days of beard stubble while waiting for the last of the hot water to reach the second floor.

Pearl spoke softly as he began applying his straight razor to his chin. "Wanna thank you, Mr. Slocum, for not havin' me put in jail tonight. I figured you was gonna do it."

"I wanted to give you a second chance, Pearl."

"There's another thing. You're gonna think I'm crazy, but I ain't the least bit sorry I killed Jake. I *wanted* him to die."

"You don't have to explain. I would have killed him myself if I'd gotten the chance."

"How come you're gonna let me stay in the same hotel room with you? Looks like you'd worry I'd try to rob you again, now that you got all that money."

"I don't think you'd do it. As odd as it sounds, I trust you now."

"I'm glad," she said, smiling, " 'cause I wouldn't rob you if you had all the money in the world. You're a real nice man, Mr. Slocum, an' I'm sorry I robbed you the first time, only I told you why I done it."

"I believe you," he said, scraping whiskers off his chin

as he looked in a mirror behind the tubs, so tired it was all he could do to finish shaving.

Pearl was waiting to undress until the maid came back with the last buckets of hot water. She watched Slocum shave, thinking out loud, or so it seemed.

"What did you mean when you told that marshal you won't have a problem with Sloan?" she asked a moment later.

"I'll offer him his money back for the dagger," he explained in a slightly thicker voice. "If he refuses, I'll make him a different proposition."

She waited, and when he didn't say any more she asked, "What kind of different proposition?"

His mouth became a thin line before he answered her. "The chance to stay alive" was all he said, wiping off his razor with a cotton towel, satisfied with a quick job of barbering his face for now.

They sat side by side in steaming tubs of soapy water. The soap had a lilac scent. Pearl soaped her breasts and used his razor under her arms, then scrubbed her face and washed her long blond hair. He smoked a rum-soaked cigar, sipping from the neck of a bottle of good Kentucky whiskey while he watched her bathe, resting his head against the high back of the tub contentedly, truly enjoying himself for the first time in days.

"You're a very pretty girl," he told her later, after she'd rinsed out her hair.

"Thanks, Mr. Slocum. I ain't used to hearin' nobody say that about me."

"Call me John. And you should get used to it. All you need is that nice dress we talked about, and some high-button shoes."

"You wouldn't buy 'em for me now, not after all I done to you."

"I might," he said, taking another delicious sip of whiskey, then drawing deeply on his cigar, blowing curls of smoke toward the ceiling.

She smiled, and her smile made him think about the odd twists of fate that had first brought them together as lovers, then turned them into adversaries, and now friends again. He was convinced she'd been a reluctant participant in the scheme to rob him, and he found he couldn't hold it against her.

"Would you really?" she asked. "How come?"

He thought about his answer. "Several reasons. I might not ever have found Jake without your help. And it was you who made sure he wasn't leaving Kansas City with my money when you got him behind that livery. I'd wounded him, but he was still able to run for it. Then there's the simple fact that I'd like to see you in a pretty dress, all fancied up like a high-class lady. I enjoy looking at beautiful women."

For some reason just then she wouldn't look at him, staring down at her hands. "Some woman's gonna be real lucky one of these days. When you find a woman you want to marry, she'll be the luckiest woman in the world. You've got a big heart, an' you can be the gentlest man I ever saw. You'll make some woman very happy when you make her your wife."

He chuckled. "Some men aren't the marrying kind. By the look of things, I'm one of 'em. I've never been able to settle in one place too long. I get this urge to see what's on the other side of the mountain. I can't explain it any better'n that."

"I wasn't talkin' about *me*, you know. I know you

wouldn't never marry *me*. All I was sayin' was, the right woman who can keep you is gonna be mighty lucky.''

"You'll find a good man one of these days, Pearl. Maybe you've been looking in the wrong places."

She nodded, and he could see she was in a melancholy mood because of their conversation.

"Give it time," he added. "You're young yet. The right man will come along."

Pearl stood up slowly, soap bubbles clinging to her naked breasts, flat stomach, rounded buttocks, and thighs, and he thought again how perfectly shaped she was.

"You can wear one of my spare shirts," he told her. "Pick the one you want."

She stepped out of the tub and began toweling off. Slocum was fascinated by her nakedness, although he was sure he was too tired to experience her charms tonight. This had certainly been one of the longest days of his life.

She lay naked beside him in the darkness, curled into a ball in his arms under a thin linen sheet. A cool breeze came from an open window beside the bed. Her hair smelled of lilacs, and her soft skin was a delight to touch as he held her.

"I'll make you feel good before we go to sleep," she offered in a whisper, reaching for his limp cock, touching it gently with her fingers.

In spite of her soft skin and loveliness he felt himself drifting off to sleep. "Maybe in the morning," he mumbled as he slipped closer to slumber, aided by the whiskey he'd consumed tonight.

His last conscious thought was of Jake Willow, lying in a pool of blood with his backbone jutting through a hole in his shirt, digging shaky fingers into the dirt while he fought his pain. Dale Moss's death was avenged. Now all that remained of unfinished business was to see a man named Sloan.

his dart, driving sharp fangs into the dust with the deadly
jaws wide. Once coiled, it would strike again, striking fo...
harder or infinitude had swept her...

21

A huge apelike man standing well over six feet introduced himself as Byron Sloan. He had a milky left eye that stared off into space, sightless. "What can I do for you, mister?" he asked as he stood behind a glass jewelry counter displaying rings and watches and necklaces of gold and silver. Sloan looked to be in his early forties, a mountain of muscle with a barrel chest and ham-sized hands, though his belly overlapped his belt and Slocum knew his stomach would be soft.

Slocum took three hundred dollars in currency from his pants pocket and placed it on the countertop. "This is your money," he began, speaking softly, evenly, staring into Sloan's good eye. "You bought an antique Mongol dagger from a fella with a scar on his face yesterday. It was stolen from me. Take your money and give me my dagger back."

Sloan's face twisted. "You must be mistaken. Now take this money and get out of my store."

Slocum shook his head very slowly. "It ain't gonna work like that. Give me the knife and take the money. No argument. No more discussion."

Sloan's powerful shoulder muscles bunched in anger.

"You don't have real good hearing, stranger. I said you were mistaken and I want you out of my store immediately. Go, or I'll throw you out."

Slocum's jaw tightened. "I can promise you that'd be a man-sized job, Mr. Sloan. The man you bought the dagger from is dead this morning. A bullet broke his spine in half last night. Give me the dagger and take your money. I've asked you real nice, but I won't ask again."

Sloan leaned forward menacingly, jutting his chin. "All that tough talk doesn't scare me, mister. I'll be the one who's breaking you in half unless you leave my place of business right now." His right hand disappeared behind his back, and Slocum was sure Sloan was reaching for a weapon.

With all the speed of experience and quick reflexes, Slocum jerked out his Colt .44, bringing it up just as Sloan came out with a pistol from his waistband. The muzzle of Slocum's gun touched the flesh under Sloan's jaw first, at an angle that would put a bullet through his brain.

Sloan froze with his pistol in midair, his eye rounding. He glanced down at Slocum's pistol, then back to his face.

"Drop it," Slocum snarled, "or I'll scatter the top of your head all over this ceiling. It'll take a good cleaning lady all day to clean up the mess."

He could see Sloan figuring his chances, poised with his revolver above the jewelry case.

"I never tell a man anything twice," Slocum said between teeth clenched in anger. "Drop the fucking gun or I'll decorate your ceiling with blood and brains."

Perhaps it was the tone of Slocum's voice, or the look in his eyes, that warned Sloan of imminent death. He slowly lowered his pistol, placing it on the countertop, his lone functioning eye glued to Slocum's face, eyelids twitching nervously.

"That's a good boy," Slocum said, taking the Pocket Model Smith and Wesson with his left hand, tucking it behind his belt. "You made a very wise choice, Mr. Sloan. Take a deep breath of fresh air, because it oughta taste sweet. If you hadn't put the gun down, there wasn't gonna be any more air for you. Now let's you and me walk real slow to the back, or wherever you've got my dagger. You're gonna give it to me and I'm leaving your money right where it is."

Sloan swallowed, yet remained silent and made no move to walk toward the rear of his shop.

"One more thing," Slocum added, holding his Colt steady against Sloan's throat. "If you sneeze, or wiggle the wrong way, I promise you I'll kill you. I've seen about all of Kansas and Kansas folks I ever care to see, so I'm in something of a hurry. But I'll stay long enough to piss on your grave if you try to trick me. A forty-four makes a hell of a hole, damn near big enough to toss a tomcat through. Just get me my dagger and take back your money. It's that simple, and we'll save the county a funeral expense."

"I'll send for the law the second you leave," Sloan said in a coarse growl.

"I doubt it. I talked to Marshal Young last night, since I knew this was where Jake Willow sold the stolen dagger. He told me he'd had suspicions about your activities for a long time. So you notify the marshal if you want. But the one thing you'd better not do is give me any problems right now getting back my property. It's a very valuable antique, but you've got to ask yourself if it's worth dying for. Now back away real slow, and head for that back door. I'll be right behind you, and if anything goes wrong, you'll hear this little cracking noise when my slug passes through your head, but you'll never hear the bang of gunpowder, or the screaming noises you're gonna make. You'll be dead, like a pile of fresh pig shit. I hope you won't test me to see if I'm telling you the truth.''

"You could be bluffing."

Slocum stood rock-still, his feet spread apart, holding his gun to Sloan's neck with a steady hand. "Just one way I know of to find out," he replied. Sloan was stalling, thinking of a way to jump him.

"You'll never get away with this. I'll send somebody after you. I know the right people."

Slocum lost his temper all at once, snaking out his left hand to seize a fistful of Sloan's brown hair, pulling his gun back just a fraction in the same swift motion. With all his strength he slammed Sloan's face downward, shattering the glass top of the counter into hundreds of pieces and shards when the huge man's head struck the counter. Flying glass shot in every direction, making an almost musical tinkling that quickly was joined by Sloan's shriek.

"My eye! My eye!" he screamed, staggering backward as both hands flew to his bloody face.

"Send anybody you want!" Slocum bellowed, wild with rage, momentarily out of control. He hurried around the remnants of the glass case and swung the barrel of his Colt across the top of Sloan's skull, making a heavy whacking noise when iron landed on skin and bone with tremendous force.

Sloan sank to his knees, his jaw agape. His hands fell to his sides while he was toppling forward, falling face-first on bits of broken glass covering the floor, out cold.

Slocum stormed to the rear door and kicked it open, still holding his pistol. In a small room at the back of the building he saw hundreds of items spread across a wooden work-bench, and among the watches and rings and other jewelry, he saw the glint of a gold-handled knife.

He picked it up and looked at it a moment. This was the object that had started all his troubles. He held it for a time, remembering events and the death of a dear friend, then whirled and stalked back to the front of the jewelry shop.

He paused at the door long enough to toss Sloan's pistol to the floor, then walked out in bright morning sunshine to climb aboard his bay stud, satisfied that, at long last, he had everything he'd had in his possession when he'd left Springfield, Missouri.

He reined away from the shop and headed for the city marshal's office. Only then did his white-hot temper begin to cool.

"It appears you're on the level, Mr. Slocum," the marshal said, handing him a telegram. "Won't be no charges filed against the woman, 'less you file 'em."

"She was forced into it. I won't press charges."

"Doc Collins told me the guy she shot died sometime last night. Can't say as I've ever seen nobody's backbone busted in half like that before."

"He earned it. He was a thief and a murderer, according to Marshal Heck Thomas, only nobody could get the goods on him for a trial."

"Did you ask Sloan about that old knife you said was stolen from you?"

"I did." Slocum had left it in his saddlebags before he came inside.

"What did the one-eyed bastard say about it? My money says he claimed he didn't know a thing about your knife."

"He denied having it. We had a minor disagreement over

who was telling the truth. There was a little scuffle. I found the dagger in his back room.''

"A little scuffle? Byron Sloan's a big son of a bitch an' tough as boot leather. I don't see nary a scratch on your hide anywhere."

"It wasn't much, really. If I remember right he tripped on something and fell on his face. There was some broken glass and he may have been cut. Nothing serious. I left the money he paid Jake Willow for the dagger and walked out with my property. If you need verification as to who truly owns it, you can contact Mr. Bradford Thomas in Springfield."

"Your word's good enough, Slocum." Marshal Young appeared to be appraising him. "You don't look all that tough to me, but any man who can handle Byron Sloan has gotta have gumption and a hell of a lot of nerve."

Slocum felt an almost irresistible itch to be riding out of Kansas City now. With his stud in bad trail shape after the hard treatment Willow gave it, he'd inquired at the railroad depot as to arrangements for putting the bay in a cattle car stall full of bedding straw and taking the train to Fort Smith. There was still the question of what to do about the girl, what she would do or where she meant to go. He replied to the marshal's remark. "Maybe I just caught Sloan on a bad day. If you've got enough information for your report I'll be leaving town now," he said.

"Suits me. I've got no more questions." Young offered Slocum his hand.

Pearl was waiting for him in the hotel room, wearing a new yellow dress and high-top leather shoes. She had a small handbag, and there were tied ribbons in her hair.

"You look beautiful," he told her, which was the truth.

She had a youthful innocence about her that belied her unfortunate past. He closed the door behind him. At dawn they'd made frenzied love for more than an hour, he recalled vividly. When her passion was awakened she had a genuine hunger for stiff cock, and she could have a seemingly unlimited number of climaxes.

"Thank you, sir," she said, giving him a mock curtsy, "and thank you for the dress. I had eight dollars left over. It's there on the dresser."

"We're free to leave Kansas City now," he said. "I talked to Marshal Young and there won't be any charges against either of us. Do you have any idea where you want to go?"

"You mean I can't go with you, don't you?"

He came over and sat on the edge of the bed. "You need a life of your own. I'm not ready to settle down. I can't take you with me to Colorado, but you can ride the train with me back to Fort Smith, and maybe I can convince Myra to give you your job again, after I explain things to her."

She shook her head. "I don't want no more of Fort Smith," she told him, a tiny tear forming in the corner of each eye. "If I can't go wherever you're goin', I reckon I'll find a way to get to Saint Louis somehow. I worked in a little bakery there a few years ago. Maybe I can get a job there. There was this boy with freckles who was real nice to me."

"I'll pay for your train ticket to Saint Louis."

She edged closer to him. "Are you right sure you wouldn't let me go with you? I'd do everything you told me to without no complainin'."

"I'm sorry, Pearl," he said, taking her hand, holding it a moment. "I'm not sure I can make you understand."

She dried her eyes with a fingertip. "I think I do understand. There's some men who just can't be satisfied with one woman."

"That may be a part of it," he admitted.

"You'd get tired of me after a spell."

"It isn't that, really. It's like I told you before about wanting to know what's on the other side of the mountain. When I see a pretty lady, I can't help wondering what she's got hidden under her skirt."

Pearl chuckled, hearing this. "Don't suppose I oughta blame you for that."

"It's a part of my nature, seems like. I get curious to see a beautiful body, like yours, only they're all a little different in various ways. I never thought of it as being wrong, to want to experience a different woman now and then."

She sat down beside him, resting her head on his shoulder. "You'll find the right woman one of these days. I only wish it could be me."

He wasn't quite sure what to say to her then. He squeezed her palm.

"If you ever get to Saint Louis you could look me up," she said softly. "I'd be glad to show you what's under my skirt any time you want."

It was his turn to laugh. He put his arm around her. "I'd never go through Saint Louis without looking you up and asking," he replied. Then he reached for the buttons at the back of her dress and began to open them slowly, kissing the soft flesh of her neck.

22

He led the bay stud slowly down a cattle loading ramp into a shipping pen on a rail siding at Fort Smith. After he saw to the horse's care at the livery stable, he'd pay a call on Myra Shirley to finish what he'd started weeks ago. And to save his good bay a long distance carrying a rider, Slocum would take trains all the way to Denver. The stud was still sore-footed and covered with spur marks from Willow's rough handling.

It was dark in Fort Smith as he led the animal to the stable and paid for its keep, yet still early enough that he expected to find Myra at home before going to the Powderkeg.

Carrying his saddlebags and wearing a new Stetson he'd bought in Kansas City, Slocum trudged down quiet streets to the address he remembered for Miss Shirley. Delivering the gift from Bradford Thomas was his first order of business. Then he meant to hire a hotel room after a sooty train ride and take a hot bath before going to bed.

Walking toward Myra's, he remembered Pearl's tearful good-bye at the railroad depot. He'd promised her again that he would visit her when he was in Saint Louis, should business ever take him there. In his heart, Slocum felt sorry for

Pearl, and had he not been made the way he was, he might have taken her with him to Denver. But he knew himself too well for that. His wanderings were not limited to seeing other parts of the country. When the right beautiful woman came along, lust for her body always got the best of him. Pearl wanted a settled man in her life, and if there was one thing Slocum had never been, it was the settling kind.

He saw lights behind Myra's windows, and walked up steps to her porch, rapping lightly with his knuckles.

"Who is it?" a woman's voice asked.

"John Slocum. I've got something for you from Brad Thomas, only it took a little longer to get it here than I figured."

She opened the door a moment later, smiling, wearing a thin black dressing gown. "Do come in, Mr. Slocum," she said as she stepped back to admit him. "I was sure Pearl and Cut Face had gotten away, or even worse, done you in. Heck Thomas told me he got a wire from Kansas City explaining what happened, asking to verify who you were and things like that. I was so relieved to hear you were okay. Please sit here in the parlor and I'll get you a glass of good whiskey. Your preference is for sour-mash Kentucky, I recall."

He pulled off his hat as she closed the door. "You've got a good memory," he told her, looking her up and down, wondering how he could have forgotten how stunningly beautiful she was, with coal-black hair and milky white skin, a tiny waist, and an oversized pair of jiggling breasts almost as large as the crown of his Stetson.

He placed his saddlebags on the floor and took out the gold dagger, offering it to her. "Before I take that kind offer of a drink and a chair, I'd like to give you this."

She took it, staring at its exquisite craftsmanship and the

goldsmithing in its ivory handle. "It's beautiful," she said in a whisper. Then her expression turned hard when she looked up at Slocum. "And that little bitch Pearl stole it from you before you could deliver it. I hope she got what she deserved."

"It wasn't entirely her doing," he explained. "It's a long story, but if you'd care to hear it, I'll tell you how she got involved, and why she's free and on her way to Saint Louis on the train."

"Saint Louis?" Myra exclaimed, allowing the front of her gown to fall open a little more, showing off a substantial amount of her cleavage as though she wasn't aware of it. "I'll get you that drink and you can tell me all about it. Please sit down. I will only be a minute in the kitchen." She examined the dagger again, moving closer to an oil lamp. "This is one of the most intricate, beautiful things I've ever seen. I must send word to Bradford to express my gratitude." She put the knife down on a coffee table, watching Slocum now. "And of course I'll have to find a way to thank you for making sure it wound up where Brad intended it to go." She smiled provocatively, then covered the cleft between her pendulous breasts and disappeared into a back room, hips swaying in a most delightful way.

He took a cushioned chair in the parlor and sat back with a sense of relief. The ancient warlord's dagger was in the right hands now. He'd kept his word to Bradford, which was what mattered most, since there are times when a man's word is all he has.

Myra leaned forward in a chair across from his as soon as he finished his story, her brow lightly furrowed in thought. "So it wasn't really Pearl's fault after all. She was so afraid to disobey Jake Willow that she was willing to do whatever he told her to.''

"That's about the size of it. She was orphaned at a very young age, and from what she told me, she's had a string of bad experiences ever since.''

"Some people are the victims of circumstances, John. They always seem to come up the loser.''

"Pearl was one of them, only I think she's on the right track now and she knows what it's like to take up with the wrong kind of man. It happened to her twice, but both times she was in desperate straits, alone and penniless. It was hard for me to blame her for what she did after I heard her sad story.''

"That was very generous of you, buying her a dress and shoes and a ticket to Saint Louis, with enough money for a rooming house and food after she got there. I hardly know you, but its obvious you're a very kindhearted man.'' Myra took a sip of brandy, licking her full lips afterward. Then she stared deeply into his eyes, a slight smile tugging the corners of her mouth. "I'm a very plainspoken woman, John. I've been noticing how you have been looking at my bosom every now and then. Would you care to see more of me?''

He couldn't halt his grin in time, for it came reflexively. "I would. I'm sure you've been told you're a very beautiful woman a thousand times. When I first saw you, I understood why Brad would send you an expensive gift, for you are indeed one of the most remarkably beautiful women I've ever seen. I'd be a fool to decline an offer like yours. In fact, I was working my way toward asking the same thing myself, only I didn't want to offend you with an improper advance.''

She stood up, placing her glass on the table. Then she

opened the front of her silky gown to reveal the fullness of her naked body underneath, generous hips below a small waist, made to appear even smaller by the tremendous size of her breasts. "I believe in asking for things I want, John," she said in a husky voice. "Life has taught me not to be a bystander. I wanted you on that first night you came to Fort Smith, but as you know all too well, things got in the way."

"I had a responsibility to get that dagger back, and they took all my money. But in many ways you and I are the same when it comes to things we want. We go after them."

She held out her hand. "Follow me to my bedroom, John. I can assure you you won't be disappointed."

Slocum stood up and tossed back the last of his drink. "I'm quite sure I won't be, Myra. I'm a pretty good judge of things like that. I've known a woman or two in my time, but I can honestly say I've never seen one any more desirable than you."

Rolling her shoulders, she let her gown fall to the floor. "Come with me, John. I hope you're well rested after your long and difficult trip to Kansas City, because I have plans for you that will require plenty of energy and I intend for it to last all night."

"I'll do my best," he promised, feeling the beginnings of a throbbing erection bulge in the crotch of his pants as he made to follow her into a side room.

Myra happened to glance down. "Dear Lord," she whispered when she noticed the swelling. "Can it be as big as all that?"

He shrugged. "Bigger'n some, I'm sure, and maybe smaller than some others."

She released his hand and unfastened the top button of his pants, anticipation behind her growing smile. She reached into his trousers and closed her fingers around the base of his cock. "It's huge," she sighed breathlessly, her breasts swaying on her rib cage when she pulled his prick out, resting it in her palm. "Now I know you'll need plenty of staying power tonight," she added, admiring his length and girth, her nipples hardening at the mere sight and feel of it. "You were built to satisfy a woman. Sam will have to handle business at the Powderkeg on his own. Some things are more important than selling whiskey."

He followed her into the bedroom after she released her grip on his cock, ready for a long night ride of a different kind than the one that had taken him across the empty plains of Kansas Territory to Kansas City.

Myra was right. There were some things more important than selling whiskey or just about anything else.